Shadows

Of The Mortal Realm

By: Shay Lee Giertz

SHADOWS OF THE MORTAL REALM
By Shay Lee Giertz

Published by Late November Literary
Winston Salem, NC 27107

ISBN (print): 978-1-7375561-5-2

*Scripture Reference taken from Revelation 12:7-8, King James
Version, public domain.

Dedication

To my parents and siblings. What a great and crazy family we have! All my love.

~Shay Lee

Author's Note

Shadows of the Mortal Realm is a work of fiction geared for young adult readers and older. Although I take great care to write clean fiction, some content—due to scary settings, elements, and characters—may not be suitable for readers under the age of sixteen.

Reader discretion is advised.

And there was war in heaven:
Michael and his angels fought against
the dragon; and the dragon fought and his angels,
and prevailed not; neither was their place found
any more in heaven.

*The Book of Revelation chapter 12, verses 7 & 8**

1

It Begins

One final push and the mother's agony was over. Everything seemed to pause as if the universe took notice and held its breath. The baby's wail pierced that moment, ringing in the ears of those who listened. And there were those who were.

The young mother smiled tiredly, as her husband kissed her sweat-soaked forehead. Neither they nor the midwife could see the horrendous demon glowering in the doorway.

"Take it. And kill it," the demon said, for it was not alone.

The shadow along the doorway contorted as a young man stepped out of it. But he paused as if unsure of what to do next.

"That's an order, Shadow." The demon towered over him.

Shadows looked deceptively human. Their black orbs for eyes were their only distinguishable mark of being a soldier of the Underworld. They often accompanied demons because they were needed for moving in and through shadows. In the mortal realm, shadows were entry points into the human conscience. Not that any of it mattered. Shadows were slaves. They did what they were told, or they died.

Still, he watched the baby in awe. Watched as the midwife cleaned the crying child. Watched as the child balled hands into little fists and wailed, subsiding only when swaddled in a blanket and placed in the arms of the mother.

Something stirred in the Shadow. Not just awe. But fear. "Is this the one?" he whispered as if the humans in the room could hear.

The demon's bulk was a looming contrast to the thin Shadow soldier. Whereas the Shadow appeared human-like, except for his eyes, the demon appeared anything but human. With blood-red skin covered in festering sores, razor-sharp teeth, and a sharp point where a nose would be, it was his massive claws and talons for feet that separated him from the lower ranks.

Now he stared at the Shadow in contempt. "We're not taking the chance. Kill it."

"But Drakkon said..."

"Last time, Drakkon got it wrong."

"Yes, but the time before that ended mankind for thousands of years."

The demon stretched his claws and clicked his talons against the floor, quietly studying the child.

The Shadow knew that the demon—although a master general—had no authority to go over Drakkon's head. Just the same, the demon's talons dripped with hell's poison and would disintegrate him with one fatal piercing. With caution, he said, "If we kidnapped the baby, we could hide it from the truth. Train it as one of our own."

"It's human," the demon spat out the words.

The Shadow never felt hopeful. That was a useless emotion of the mortal realm. But in this moment, as he stared at the child, he felt something. Something he'd never felt before. Something like hope. "Yes, but the baby's an anomaly. You know as well as anyone that it can access both realms. It could train in the Shadow ranks."

"The Shadow ranks? Train alongside the likes of you?"

The Shadow knew to tread carefully. "Just so it can be observed. If its abilities are truly unmatched, then Drakkon will find other uses. But we should try."

The demon turned on him quickly. Picked up the Shadow soldier with his demon claws. His hot breath—the breath of hell—singed the soldier's insides. "You are nothing but a slave," he said, slowly and menacingly. "If we were to take it, the last place I would put it is with the likes of you."

The Shadow tried one more time. "But if we kill it, we kill any hope of escaping our prison."

The demon released the thin soldier. "And if it chooses the other side? Even if it is an anomaly, it's still human, and humans have the ultimate weapon. Free will."

The Shadow had no answer.

"It's dangerous, and it needs to die. Step into the mother's thoughts and get her to set it down. Have the other humans leave the room. I will kill it myself."

The Shadow stiffly nodded. He understood that he must follow orders or die. He stepped into the shadow of the young woman and disappeared. Once in the shadow, the soldier could step into the minds of the humans. It was so simple. Normally, he didn't hesitate. But this wasn't exactly a normal situation.

The demon sensed the Shadow's hesitation. "Do it. That's a command." He watched as the mother blinked and kissed the baby's head, pulling it away from the milk. The baby's eyes were closed, as the young woman wrapped the blanket tighter around it.

"Here," she said to the father. "The baby should rest."

The demon caught the faint shifting of light as the Shadow moved from one shadow to another.

"Yes," the midwife agreed. "As should you. Swallow this pain reliever to take the edge off." She handed the mother a cup of water and two pills.

The father, who had been holding the child, set the child down. He kissed the baby, then kissed the mother. "I will be right back. I'm going to call the family."

"It's done," The Shadow said to the demon, walking over to him.

Within minutes, the midwife and father had left the room, and the young mother had dozed off to sleep. The demon with his poisonous talons expanded his blood-red wings and lifted himself up, taking up nearly every inch of the room's capacity.

The Shadow looked away. Hell's only hope of escaping the last couple thousand years of bondage was about to be murdered.

2

Twenty Years Later

Marcy concentrated on the shampoo bottles. One promised hair as smooth as silk, but the green bottle guaranteed stronger hair in two weeks or your money back. Not that Marcy cared too much about the money part. She stole every human item she owned. But still, the green bottle had a delicious fruity scent.

The last customer of the night left the drug store. Marcy had to be careful. Unlike other Shadows, humans could see her. She grabbed a bottle of both shampoos, stuffed them inside her jacket, zipped it up, and stepped into a shadow. At least when inside shadows, she was protected, but she didn't like staying in them for long. Other Shadows welcomed the darkness, but not Marcy. Now as she stepped out of the shadow, she stood on the sidewalk of the store, looking in.

Kraal said she was the best shifter of all the Shadows. He said it with pride when no one else was around to hear it. In front of others, he scolded her for taking human paraphernalia. She tried to listen for Kraal's sake. He explained, "The punishment could be severe, and not just for you. I would face punishment too."

"No one even notices," she complained.

"Here in hell, we're nothing," Kraal warned her. "But that

doesn't mean no one notices. We are far more numerous than any other demon faction. It may take a while to be noticed, but if you are not careful, you *will* be noticed."

"Why is that such a bad thing? And if there are so many of us, can't we handle whatever is thrown at us? There's power in numbers."

"We may be many, but because we are part human, we can die easily. Every demon in hell knows it. We are slaves to Guardians. The wrong move will get you disintegrated. The quicker you learn that, the safer you will be."

So, she tried to follow the rules. But night after night, it was the same mundane activities. Practice dream-weaving and thought-manipulation on unsuspecting mortals. Which meant she needed to shake things up now and then. She just couldn't help herself. Human materials fascinated her.

She moved from shadow to shadow until she stood in front of the house where her services were required. She might not enjoy moving undetected in the mortal realm, but when she stepped into a shadow, it allowed her and other Shadows to travel in such a way it defied the mortal laws. That's how she became so good at stealing. Step into a shadow and magically disappear.

Oh, how she wished she could disappear from this stupid trainee assignment. She was already bored. It was as if she could hear Kraal reciting in her head, "The Shadow's primary job is to control mortals' thoughts. It starts with dreams. Since you're only a Shadow trainee, you will only manipulate the dreams of low-risk humans, just to get a feel for it. However, don't ever forget how important dream-weaving is. Once you finish your training, you will be in charge of manipulating much more significant mortals."

"Yeah, yeah, yeah," she muttered as she stared at the house. There were three simple rules to being a Shadow trainee that Kraal made her recite often: Stay undetected, don't delve too deep into human memory, and leave human course unaltered.

All of which Marcy had broken. And more than once.

Tonight, it would be no exception. Rules were simply made to be broken. Other Shadow trainees—and there had to be millions of them—followed the rules. Period. She hadn't met one to defy anything that was given to them as an order. Even Mathilde, her young friend, followed the rules. She longed not to, but when push came to shove, she did what she was told. So, that left all the mischief to Marcy.

Once in the house, she finished the dream sequence on the mortal woman, mixing new encounters with hodge-podge from an assortment of files. She laughed to herself. "Sorry, lady," she murmured. "You'll wake up thinking you had way too much Mexican food last night." Once she stepped out of the woman's shadow, she continued working through the other four humans in the house. She stepped from one room to another, the night aiding in her invisibility.

Marcy cringed when she reached the ransacked room of a teenage male. She hated even peeking at the memories of males, but teenage males were by far the worst. Ugh. She stepped into his shadow, blinked, and stood in his central circuitry system located in the inner-compartments of the brain. She had been told most Elder Shadows could manipulate thoughts of any human within a thousand-foot radius just by standing in a single shadow.

That'd be nice. Unfortunately, she was only a Shadow trainee. Kraal wouldn't let her master the skill.

The teenage boy's brain activity already worked in a frenzy. Marcy shuddered in disgust. "Okay, you don't need my help, big guy. Have fun."

She stepped quickly out of his shadow, grateful that some humans had active imaginations and didn't require Shadow assistance all the time.

"Psst, Marcy? You finished?"

Marcy walked into the hallway and spotted Mathilde at the top of the stairs. Mathilde looked like any normal twelve-year-old human. She currently sported twin blonde braids that dangled over her slender shoulders, and her bangs were getting a little too long and nearly covered her eyes. Marcy knew her mentee did it for a distinct reason. It was easy to cover the one identifiable marking when it came to Shadows: complete black orbs for eyes. Everything. The iris, the retina, they were so black they mirrored like glass. This was the reason for rule #1. If a human was to stare into the black abyss of a Shadow's eyes, they would see their worst fears. But Marcy, for some strange, unknown reason, had regular human-like eyes. So, she had no problem breaking that rule.

"I'm hungry," Mathilde was saying as they skirted from one

shadow into a looming streetlight shadow outside. Marcy stepped out of it and materialized to be visible in the mortal world. "You promised me a burger, but we won't be able to go tonight."

"We can make it work. Where's everyone else? They'll want to come too," Marcy said and searched the shadows. A Shadow's eyesight saw everything in the mortal and spirit world, whether she had materialized into visibility or not. And in one way, all the Shadows were the same: they could eat and enjoy human food. "No one's around."

"They're all with the Guardian," Mathilde said and rolled her eyes. "Like I was saying, I don't think we'll be able to do our little side trip."

"Hagar is easy to ditch."

"It's not Hagar. It's a new one. He looks scary."

"All Guardians look scary. They're supposed to so that we'll listen to them. And who looks scarier than Hagar? That guy has three eyes and four arms."

"There is something about the new one. And he's asking for you."

Marcy crinkled her nose. "Am I the last one to finish?"

"Yes, but that's because you had to get some more shampoo."

"Oh, that reminds me. Hide these in your jacket." Marcy handed Mathilde the shampoo bottles. "I might need the space for burgers."

Mathilde shoved the shampoos in her jacket and zipped it up, looking unconvinced. "Well, I'd at least check in with him. He's asking for you, and he doesn't look happy."

Why would a Guardian ask for her? Marcy wondered if she'd been found out. "Keep your jacket zipped, and your hands in your pockets. If he's wanting me, then stay in the background. Got it?"

Mathilde nodded. "Be careful."

Guardians could stop a Shadow permanently. That's why they were chosen to be escorts. To make sure the Shadows came back. Kraal had told her once that Shadows were part descendants of humans. They couldn't allow a Shadow to linger in the mortal world; it could alter the course of all existence. But Marcy had never been told why. What she did know was that Guardians controlled fire. This made them powerful and dangerous.

She'd heard the stories. How the burning starts on the inside and builds until implosion. She'd seen Shadows with burn marks or even missing limbs. Shadows who went too far. But they were few and far between. Most Shadows followed their Guardians' orders. Did their job. Blah, blah, blah.

The thought of being subject to a Guardian for eternity deflated her mood. This wasn't the destiny she wanted. So, she tested the waters a bit. Broke the rules. If for no other reason than to break the monotony of Shadow existence.

If it was up to Marcy, she'd stay in the mortal realm forever. The mortal world wasn't perfect, but parts of it were. And the air. The energy. It was so palpable. The earth seemed to thrum in harmony with the heartbeats of its occupants. But it wasn't a thought Marcy took seriously. Guardians answered to one commander: Drakkon. He said no Shadows inhabit the mortal realm, and that was that.

"There you are," one of the trainees said to Marcy, as she and Mathilde approached. "What did you do?"

"I haven't done anything yet, why? What's going on?"

"This Guardian ordered Hagar to leave and that he would take it from here. When Hagar started to argue with him, he killed him."

Marcy's throat seized in terror. "Killed him? A Guardian killed another Guardian?"

The boy nodded. "And he's been asking all of us about you. He's angry, Marcy. Did you do something?"

Marcy peeked around the boy and saw the Guardian looming in the dark recesses of the dilapidated bridge. As if sensing her, he turned and marched over to Marcy, as the Shadow trainees cleared his path.

Marcy tried to even out her breathing, but his intense stare and furious expression seemed to burn her insides. He stopped directly in front of her. Marcy only came to his chin, so she had to tilt her head back to keep eye contact. She tried not to be revolted. Scars covered his entire body. From his head down to his arms and fingers, he was completely disfigured from the scars. For a brief moment, his eyes burned from a raging red to the deepest of blues. But the raging red quickly resurfaced. "Marcy?" His deep voice reverberated in her head. It seemed familiar. Had she heard it before?

"Yes," she squeaked. "Whatever I did, I can explain."

His stare intensified. He somehow was transferring his raging fire inside of her because it burned so badly, she doubled over.

"Stop. Please."

"Marcy!" Mathilde called.

"Stay back!" The Guardian roared. He grabbed Marcy's arm and jerked it. "Look at me."

Marcy couldn't help it, she whimpered.

"Look at me, you wretched creature!" When she did, she saw the fire ignite in his eyes. In a flash, he grabbed her other forearm and squeezed with the strength of a giant. Marcy yelped in pain, as the fire glowed in his eyes like a red haze and traveled through her body tearing at her insides. She would have fallen to her knees, but his grip only tightened paralyzing her with internal flames.

She vaguely heard the trainees' protests. Then she saw the Guardian's mouth. He seemed to be saying something.

She thought of Mathilde for an instant, and something inside her stirred until an energy stormed through her, pounding the fire with resistance.

Let me go, she thought with such force that a current ripped through them sending Marcy catapulting across the pavement.

She lay flat on her back and fought to catch her breath. Her head felt like nails had been drilled into it, and her body still seemed paralyzed.

"Marcy, are you okay?" Mathilde's face hovered over hers distressed.

"I can't move," she managed to say.

"How are you still alive is the question," Arec—another senior trainee—commented on her other side. "You should be pulverized.

I watched his eyes intensify. You should be nothing but ash right now. Can you move now?"

Her toes and fingers tingled like a cooling salve had been applied. "I feel my fingers and toes," she said. "What are you doing to them?"

"Nothing," he said. "Why?"

"It feels like a cooling agent has been applied and is working through my body."

Mathilde and Arec stared at her strangely.

"You should be dead," Arec said again.

"How many times are you going to say that?" Mathilde asked annoyed.

Arec kept his eyes on Marcy. "I want to know what's going on. Why were you able to throw Lynde off of you? How? None of this makes sense."

"I don't know," she said. "Where is he?"

"On the other side of the bridge," Mathilde whispered with a wicked grin. "He's sitting up, but he hasn't stood to his feet yet."

Arec snorted a chuckle. "Should I go check on him? Chances are his ego needs tending to, especially with a name like Lynde."

Marcy could now feel the sensation of her heart beating. She wiggled her fingers and toes. Moved her limbs. Then tentatively sat up. "Wow," she said as she gazed at her forearm where Lynde had squeezed. Smoke came off her flesh, but the skin remained intact. "No scar?"

"Something weird is going on," Arec said to her. "Maybe you're different in other ways than just your eyes."

"That would be so cool," Mathilde could hardly contain her glee. "Teach me how to do that."

The other Shadow trainees had gathered around her but didn't approach her other than to touch her forearm. Arec helped her stand, and the trainees watched in awe at the sight.

Then Lynde towered over them, his face relatively calm, but the fire in his eyes gave away his fury. "Let's go," he ordered and extended his hand again.

"Are you going to tell us what happened?" Mathilde asked him. "How did Marcy push you away?"

Lynde's features contorted to match the fury of the flames. "Marcy did nothing," he spat out her name like rancid acid. "I forced myself to release her before she became a burnt lamb chop. Any other questions?"

Mathilde turned to Marcy and whispered in her ear, "I take it a burger's out of the question."

Marcy was still shaken and not entirely herself. Her limbs hung like limp noodles, and even a burger didn't tempt her. She shook her head at Mathilde, who squeezed Marcy's hand in understanding.

"Let's go back," Marcy managed to say. "We'll do our training exercises another time."

Arec and Mathilde supported Marcy on either side as the rest of the trainees walked through the blue mist. The trio started to walk through when a low growl stopped Marcy. She turned and saw

Lynde watching her, but his eyes kept shifting from deep blue to raging red.

"Hurry," Marcy whispered to the other two. They quickly walked into the blue mist and away from a dangerous Guardian.

3

New Orders

The wind blew with such intensity power lines went down and trees fell to the ground. The sky had turned an angry gray as the torrential rain began. Screams filled the air, and Tor watched as the humans ran for shelter. Not that it would save them. He had made sure of that.

The massive hurricane would flood hell with new arrivals. That should make Drakkon happy, or at the very least, get him off Tor's back.

"Did you finish your assignments?" he asked the Elder Shadow assigned to him.

"Yes," Kraal said. "Are we ready?"

Tor turned to Kraal. They'd worked together a few times. Tor preferred to work alone, but Drakkon often insisted that an Elder Shadow follow along. Probably as a spy, but Tor didn't care either way. Most Shadows were disgusting and easily turned into nightmares. They were the lowest ranks, merely slaves among the masses of demons and Guardians, and Tor had no use for them. But out of all of them, Kraal was the easiest to work with. "Our work here is done."

Tor extended his arm and formed the blue mist. The two stepped through it. And they came face-to-face with Drakkon. Human cultures had different names for him, but in these parts, he was simply Drakkon, the evilest of beings. He could shift into two forms: one as a human form and one as a dragon form. He currently faced Tor as a well-groomed human.

Most of Tor's memories consisted of Drakkon. Tor had not existed for millennia like the other hell inhabitants. He had been a child. Somehow, he was part human, not that anyone told him how that came to be. But he grew up trained and tortured by Drakkon. Now he was the mightiest of the Underworld's Guardians, and supposedly Drakkon's pride and joy. But that meant nothing to Tor. He knew that Drakkon could turn on him in a moment.

"I have new orders for you," Drakkon said. "There's a Shadow trainee causing problems."

"So?" Tor curled his lip in disgust. "Who cares about stupid Shadow trainees?"

"This one's different. Go and keep her in line. And if that doesn't work, then kill her."

Tor felt the sudden change in atmosphere. One of his many skills, he could sense even the slightest shift of mood or tone. And it came from Kraal. Tor kept the observation to himself. "You want me to babysit a Shadow trainee?"

"She's different. Like you. It would be good to have you both by my side, but if she's too much of a headache, I don't want her. I leave it up to you." Drakkon paused, then continued, "I trust you will handle the situation." He left without waiting for a reply.

Kraal turned to Tor. "Am I free to leave?"

"What do you know about this Shadow trainee?"

"There are countless Shadows and trainees. I do not know most of them."

"You know this one. I can feel it. Now, tell me about her."

"I have heard of a Shadow trainee with blue eyes."

"Blue eyes? Like a human?"

"Yes, but that's about all I know."

Tor felt the slight shift again. "I sense there's more."

Kraal acted unphased, almost to the point that Tor nearly questioned his senses. "It is as Drakkon says, she is different, but I do not know to what extent."

"He wouldn't have me babysit some low-life trainee simply because she's different."

"It's only a rumor, sir. I don't want to worry you with it."

"I never worry. Tell me."

"The last Guardian tried to kill her and was unsuccessful."

Tor raised his eyebrows. "Unsuccessful? Shadows are scum and are easily disintegrated."

Kraal's features changed slightly, but he regained control. It was evident that Tor's words bothered him. "That's all I heard. The Guardian tried to disintegrate her, and she threw him off."

"I don't believe it." Tor dismissed the account. He sensed the truth of Kraal's statement, but he could not see any Shadow defending themselves against a Guardian or any demon for that matter. "All right, I'm intrigued. That is all, Kraal."

Kraal nodded and left quickly.

Tor scanned his surroundings, already feeling bored. He stood just inside the gargantuan gates that ushered the dead to their unfortunate destination. A pair of six-headed beasts stood at their posts. He remembered when Drakkon took him to this same location when he was much younger. He remembered how terrified and destitute the souls were and how delighted Drakkon acted. But Tor learned early on not to show any emotion or empathy toward anyone or anything. Those were weaknesses.

Now, he felt nothing. Or, at least, that's what he told himself.

Marcy

4

New Information

When Marcy opened her eyes, she had to blink the sleep away. She lay for a moment listening to her surroundings and shaking off the disorientation. The powerful roar of the waterfall outside her tent reminded her of where she was and what had happened.

Arec and Mathilde had delivered her to her tent, and she had collapsed. The rest? She had to think about the rest. First, she woke up humming again. It couldn't be from a dream. Shadows didn't dream. But she remembered a woman singing a lullaby. It was the same images as before. Over and over again.

Marcy sat up uneasy. Her clothes were still on from last night all wrinkled and musty. She peeled them off and went to the basin, grabbing a water gallon and pouring it in. The waterfall may have been beautiful and melodious in sound, but it was undrinkable. Not real water; more like an illusion of water. Marcy tried one time to cup some in her hand. It felt real, but when she pulled her cupped hands out, nothing was there. Not a drop, only vapor. Any water in Levea had to be smuggled from the mortal world. And she was the one who did most of the smuggling. Other levels of Levea had groups of Shadow trainees who didn't bathe, barely slept, and acted like animals. Marcy refused for that to happen in her group. Hell or no hell, her group had to bathe.

As she washed, the fuzziness of the previous night's events began to clarify. She scrubbed her face and saw Lynde's barely controlled fury. She opened a smuggled shampoo bottle and carefully massaged her head then leaned over to rinse out her long auburn locks, all the while replaying what happened. He had obviously been sent there for her. Kraal had warned her, but she hadn't listened. But why wasn't she dead?

She had felt it. Something inside her threw Lynde off. And she couldn't escape the fact that her body was completely unscathed by the trauma. Not to mention, she didn't feel any different. The weakness had left, and now she seemed back to normal. Arec had been right. She shouldn't have lived through that, let alone not have any scar.

"Can I come in?"

Marcy turned to the voice, then threw an oversized shirt over her head. "Yeah, all's clear."

Kraal stepped inside. "I heard about you and your antics last night. Thought I'd come and check-in."

Marcy audibly sighed in relief. "I'm so glad you're here." Marcy went over and hugged him, but he stopped her. "I'm not here for hugs. I've told you not to show affection in Levea or any other part of hell."

"Sorry. I'm just really glad to see you. Something happened."

"That's why I'm here. To find out what you did to tip off Drakkon about a Shadow trainee who needs his attention."

"A Guardian showed up and asked about me, and then he attacked me with internal fire."

"And you're still standing?" Kraal began to pace. "How is this possible?"

"I don't know what happened. He grabbed me, and I couldn't move or think. I only felt fire. Then there was this pressure inside, and the next minute, he's catapulting off of me."

Kraal lifted Marcy's arms and inspected them. "He grabbed your arm and tried to disintegrate you?"

"Yes. He said he released me, but Kraal, I don't think that's what happened. It was like a force inside of me pushed him off. Is that even possible?"

Kraal watched Marcy with a guarded expression, then again, Shadows did not give in or reveal emotions. "If he truly tried to disintegrate you, you'd be dead. He had to have released you."

"Maybe I'm different. Like my eyes. Maybe I can't be harmed by Guardians. Wouldn't that be incredible? And if I could figure out how I did it, then I could teach the trainees. We could start a Shadow army—"

"Stop it!" he hissed. His anger surprised Marcy. He had never been angry with her, not even with all of her stealing from the mortal world. Now, he checked outside the tent, then came back inside. "You cannot go around saying things like that." In a whisper, he added, "Drakkon can and will kill all of you. Without hesitation."

"But what about last night? I'm telling you that something came from inside of me."

Kraal covered her mouth with his hand. "Marcy, please stop talking. You are going to get all of us killed. And if for some strange, unexplainable reason you have some magical power that none of us have, then Drakkon will slaughter us and make you watch."

"It's about time you woke up," Mathilde teased as she came in. "Oh, hi Kraal."

"Go back outside," he ordered. Mathilde lowered her head and obeyed. He removed his hand from Marcy's mouth and whispered, "Drakkon is sending someone your way. I am risking everything by warning you. If anyone asks, we do not know each other. And if anyone asks, say that the Guardian released you. Say *nothing* about what you told me. Do you understand?"

Marcy's mind whirled. Kraal acted so angry and fearful that she wanted to obey, but a part of her revolted at the thought of acting as if nothing happened. She had never met Drakkon, even though she had heard horror stories of his evil. Would he kill all of the trainees? Would he kill Kraal? "I guess I won't say anything."

"Promise me."

"You always told me that promises meant nothing in hell."

"A promise from you means something. Now, promise me."

So, Kraal trusted Marcy to keep a promise? Then again, for Kraal, wouldn't she try? "Of course. I promise. I'll do as you say."

He seemed satisfied with Marcy's response. "I have to go. They cannot know I came to you." He slipped out and ordered Mathilde to say nothing to anyone about seeing him.

Mathilde entered. "What was that all about?"

"What do you think? I guess news spread of what happened."

"I've been waiting to talk to you, but you slept through the night and the day in the mortal realm." She turned and rezipped the flap. Mathilde had the same clothes on from the night before too, but that didn't surprise Marcy. Other Shadows didn't sleep near as much as she did. Just another area Marcy was different.

"What's wrong?" Marcy asked. The urgency in Mathilde's voice surprised her.

Mathilde's face changed to a grim expression. "I overheard stuff."

Marcy combed her hair, waiting for Mathilde to continue. She was still processing Kraal's surprise visit.

"After we dropped you off in your tent, Arec deserted me, but I wasn't tired yet, so I went to find Lynde. I wanted to see what he'd do." Mathilde sat on the edge of Marcy's cot.

"So, you don't buy his story either?" Marcy was relieved that she wasn't entirely crazy.

Mathilde shook her head. "Please. Everyone saw what happened. His face was murder, and you should have been disintegrated. No offense," she added.

"No offense taken," Marcy said. "But following a Guardian can't be safe. They're on the other side of the waterfall. How'd you even get over there?" Marcy had never even thought about going on the other side of Levea. Guardians were creepy enough, and

Kraal told her other demons were even worse. The less time she spent with them the better.

"I've been following them for a while, actually," Mathilde admitted. "I'm curious, I guess. If I'm going to have to serve one someday, I want to know what I'm getting into, you know?"

Marcy nodded, rather impressed with the girl. She had guts. Marcy smiled at her. "So, what happened?"

"There are a few bridges that can carry a Shadow over, but it has an impenetrable field. Elder Shadows pass through by some pattern they trace on it. So, I tried to follow the Elder closely and kind of slip across."

"And?"

"It didn't work. The first couple of times it'd just bounce me back. Then I realized that maybe I needed to dematerialize. So right when one walked through, I would dematerialize into a shadow of their clothing."

"But we can't access a Shadow or Guardians thoughts. They don't have shadows," Marcy tried to wrap her head around the idea that cute little Mathilde was doing all this on her own.

"They don't have shadows, but their clothes do. I wasn't trying to access their central circuitry, I only hopped aboard for a ride." Mathilde grinned rather proud of her accomplishment.

"That's incredible," Marcy complimented. "But Mathilde be careful. They can see you dematerialized too."

"A part of me thinks, they knew. I always picked new Shadows. Ones who've just joined the ranks. They're still sort of decent.

Anyway, once I'm over there, I stay in stealth mode."

"Stealth mode?" Marcy laughed. "The trainee spy reporting for duty."

"Yep," Mathilde agreed. "There's been a buzz going on lately. Drakkon's getting his legions ready for some kind of battle."

"What's that about?" Marcy felt intimidated that Mathilde knew about all this, and she was clueless. "I thought Drakkon was busy keeping peace between the two realms."

Mathilde shook her head. "I guess he hates the mortals and wants them gone."

"Gone?" Marcy's voice squeaked. She happened to find humans fascinating, and she had to be part human herself. "This doesn't make sense. You must have heard wrong." Marcy twisted her hair up and clipped it. "Mathilde, I don't know what to tell you. It sounds weird to me. How come we know nothing about any of this?"

"I don't know anymore. Other than last night. That's what I came to tell you about."

"So, you knew all this and didn't say anything?" Marcy laced up her boots.

"You didn't ask," Mathilde defended. "Anyways, Lynde said something about what happened."

Marcy stopped adjusting a belt around her waist. "Lynde? The Guardian from last night?" Her stomach rolled. She put her hand over her mouth. "This is bad."

Mathilde nodded. "He went directly to one of Zorul's men. I

don't know who. I was outside the tent. But Lynde said something like, 'There's a Shadow trainee that needs to join the ranks. She's dangerous, and she needs a tighter leash.'"

"Are you sure he was talking about me?"

"Who else could he be talking about? No other Shadow can do what you did last night."

"This Lynde guy is pushing for me to join the ranks? I'm not ready. I don't want to."

"That isn't the only thing I need to tell you. They started discussing if it would be better off to kill you so that other Shadow trainees don't get any ideas."

"Why is any of this happening? I'm a nobody Shadow trainee."

"Somehow you got the attention of an awfully powerful Guardian. Did you see his scars?"

"How could I not? They covered him." Marcy had heard enough. She unzipped the tent and stumbled to the waterfall. She tried deep breaths, but it wasn't working. Levea's atmosphere stayed thick with heat and humidity: no wind, no sun, just gray atmospheric pressure so palpable it hung like a wet blanket. She sat on the ground and hugged her knees.

"Maybe Drakkon found out that I don't want to join the ranks."

"No trainee wants to join the ranks. They turn into monsters. So, he'd want to kill all of us." Mathilde hugged her knees just like Marcy.

"Maybe it's because I steal so much stuff."

"We are the best-dressed group of Shadow trainees," Mathilde said it with pride. "But you did try to defy Lynde, or whatever his name is, and that's not the first time you've disobeyed a Guardian."

Marcy held her head in her hands. "So, the punishment is death? Or to join the ranks?"

She felt Mathilde's arms around her and turned to hug the girl. There was comfort in a hug, regardless of what Kraal said.

"I'm sorry," Mathilde said and let go. "I shouldn't have thrown it all at you at once. It was too much information boiling inside of me." She looked at Marcy strangely and wiped her face. "How do you form tears?"

Marcy hadn't realized she'd been crying. "Must be another trait of mine that makes me different."

"Your differences are beautiful," Mathilde sighed. "You don't know how many times I've wanted to cry. I've tried until my insides hurt. But nothing comes out of these alien eyes. I'm a demon just like the rest of them."

"Don't say that. Besides, tears make you weak." Marcy took in a breath of the heavy air and wiped at her face. Weakness was not something to demonstrate in hell.

"It's true about Shadow trainees being nothing but lower-level demons. I overheard that, as well. We're worse than imps; nothing more than slaves. Once we're under a Guardian, it's even worse. We do dirty work. Really, really dirty work. Mortal wars are started by Elder Shadows. They manipulate human emotions and thoughts. And if we don't obey orders, a Guardian disintegrates us." She said it so matter-of-factly that Marcy was taken aback.

"You're not a demon. I know that. You're part human, right? That's got to count for something."

"We're nothing but a bunch of outcasts who will continue to be slaves. Not exactly an eternity I'm rooting for, but…" Mathilde glanced over at Marcy, only to turn and stare at the waterfall mirage. "But there is something about you. Call me crazy, but there's something about you that scares them."

Marcy stood and reached for Mathilde's hand to help her up. "So, Lynde had every intention of killing me?"

"It sounded like it to me. Marcy, if someone higher up wants you gone, what about the rest of us?"

Marcy squeezed her eyes shut and told herself to relax. She could think her way out of anything. Before she knew it, she began to hum the lullaby from her sleep.

"Interesting music selection."

Marcy stopped and opened her eyes to a tall young man in Guardian apparel. He had the golden bandolier of a true Guardian, but he couldn't have been much older than Marcy. He might not have been as beastly as other Guardians or their apprentices, but he looked just as menacing. His black hair hung past his ears, and his eyes currently blazed orange, which enhanced the few scars he had on his face. Marcy felt a stir within her, but she couldn't tell if it was from fear or something else.

5

Introductions

She wasn't what Tor expected. All of his dealings with Shadows and their trainees did not prepare him for *her*.

It wasn't just her long, auburn hair, full lips, or slender physique. He enjoyed the female form, but it was almost commonplace anymore. But when she gazed upon him, it stopped him.

Her eyes were a pale blue that shot energy through him. At least, he thought it was energy. It burned, but not like a flame, more like an electrical current. For a moment, it took his breath. He waited for the discomfort to pass.

She was saying something. Tor tried to focus, but as long as her eyes held his, he was lost. He needed to look away but couldn't. His power came almost as much from intimidation as from control of the elements. She needed to look away first.

The energy had yet to dissipate.

Look away, he nearly screamed out loud. Tor decided to turn from her, which would allow them to break eye contact while not taking away his command. But he didn't need to because suddenly she looked over at the other trainee. The relief was immediate.

"What was that?" he asked, once he found his words.

"What was what?" she asked.

She annoyed him. Had she not felt that? But she acted oblivious to what happened. Tor decided to use it to his advantage. "What was that song? The tune you hummed sounds *human*, which is banned here. And from what I see, you seem to have a love affair going on with the mortals."

Tor stepped away from her, investigating the human paraphernalia. His entire scope of vision looked like something from a mortal's camping magazine. Tents were spread out, water jugs sat next to the tent openings, and blankets and clothes hung along clothesline and twinkle lights. "You smuggled all of this?"

"Maybe," she said from behind him. "It's not hurting anyone, and I refuse for us to live like animals."

If Tor wasn't so annoyed, he'd be impressed. "Complete disregard for authority. No wonder I was called."

"Please." Tor heard the sarcasm in her voice. "Doesn't Drakkon have other things to worry about than a Shadow trainee humming a song or smuggling some clothes?"

"Don't talk to me that way." He created fire within the palm of his hand. "It would be a shame to light that pretty long hair of yours on fire."

When she didn't speak, Tor snuck a glance. She stared at the fireball in his hand with her bottom lip trembling and took a step back.

Good, he thought. He had regained control, even if he could still feel the aftereffects of her gaze.

"Here's what's going to happen," he said, playing with the fire in his hand. "I'm going to be your Guardian tonight. I have a million other things to do, but Drakkon feels that babysitting the blue-eyed Shadow trainee on the eve before she joins the ranks is important. So, here I am. It would be a shame to kill you, so be a good little girl. Now let's get this stupid thing over with. Shall we?"

She didn't move.

He snapped his fingers at her, extinguishing the fire, then turned and walked toward the rest of the camp. "Gather whatever trainees you want to take and let's get your next expedition over with."

The younger trainee jogged to keep up with Tor. "Guardian, sir, we normally take the east coast past two o'clock in the morning mortal time and work until almost daybreak. We still have a few mortal hours. Isn't that right, Marcy?"

Tor eavesdropped. *Marcy? Her name is Marcy?* That name didn't seem to fit her.

"It's too early to go." Marcy now walked alongside him.

"Your next expedition is now. We're going to the western seaboard." Tor kept walking.

"The western seaboard will just be falling to sleep. And only a percentage of them. Many will still be up. Not to mention that's not where we've been assigned to go," Marcy said the last part slowly as if talking to a child.

Tor stopped, irritation causing flames to form. He said, "Stop talking. I issue a command, and you follow it. It's that simple." He braved another glance in her direction and felt the shock of electricity immediately, although since he anticipated it this time, he was able to manage his body's response.

As Tor continued to march toward the rest of the trainees, he overheard the younger girl whisper to Marcy. "Is it true? Are you joining the ranks? That means that tomorrow you'll be gone."

"We'll talk about it later," Marcy whispered in return.

Tor felt Marcy's internal battle for control. She seemed to struggle the most with anger and fear. But a few times, her energy shifted, and Tor sensed curiosity. She was curious about him.

Good. She could stay curious for all Tor cared. What he needed was for this assignment to be over.

6

Ditching

Marcy felt the panic weigh her down. She didn't want to join the ranks. She didn't want to swear allegiance to Drakkon. Why couldn't they just leave her on earth? And what about Mathilde? Who'd look after her? Who would make sure that she bathed, and that she didn't turn into an animal like other Shadow trainees in other groups?

The girls had to walk fast to catch up to the Guardian. As they kept going in the direction of the assembly of tents, Marcy squeezed Mathilde's hand. She couldn't let the young girl see how desperate and scared she was. When a Shadow was birthed, the child was brought to one of the levels to be raised and trained. Trainees between the mortal ages of twelve and fourteen were responsible for the upkeep of the children. Marcy was assigned Mathilde's tent five years ago, and the bond between them stayed tight. Most trainees seemed to show some human element by being kind to those children in their care. Shadow children had no parents, and what the human world took for granted, just did not exist in Levea. Luckily, children found care and some comfort in the young trainees in their charge. Marcy never forgot her senior trainee and mentor, Kraal, even though since joining the ranks, he rarely came around. Today's visit had been the first in a long time.

Marcy's heart pulled, wondering if she'd ever be able to visit Mathilde or if she would become evil and sinister like other Elder Shadows. She put the thought aside. She already had enough mixed emotions, no need for any more.

"Don't let him get to you," Mathilde whispered.

But the thoughts kept coming. Just thinking about what happened the previous night led to so many questions. How was she able to push off a Guardian? Why did that upset Drakkon? Why send this new one, and what did this mean for the trainees with her? Quiet anger brewed inside her. Something had to give, and questions needed to be answered. But Kraal made her promise, and he trusted her to keep the promise.

"Marcy?" Mathilde tugged on her hand. "The Guardian is talking to you."

Marcy quickly tuned in. He said something about the western seaboard needing a disturbance. "What kind of disturbance?"

"That is none of your business," he spat out the words. "Since my services are needed there, that is where we will be heading. Now notify these slaves, and let's get this over with."

She opened her mouth to defend the trainees but remembered her promise and decided not to stir his anger anymore than she already had. Marcy called out to the other trainees, telling them to assemble.

"What's going on? We're not supposed to leave for another couple of mortal hours," Arec said.

"We're leaving early. Guardian's orders," Mathilde said for Marcy.

"Is she okay?"

Marcy, lost in her thoughts again, snapped back to reality and noticed the other trainees gathered around her. They snuck tentative glances at the new Guardian but kept their distance. "Sorry, a bit distracted, I guess."

"Yeah, last night was crazy."

Marcy nodded. She didn't want to talk about it. "All right, let's separate across a portion of the Western seaboard today. We'll stick to Oregon, Washington, and parts of Canada."

"Canada's cold," one boy complained.

"We don't feel the cold, moron," another argued.

"Yes, we do!"

"Okay, well, we're not affected by the cold," another argued.

"Just because I won't get frostbite doesn't mean I want to frolic in the white stuff. We can still feel the cold, and I don't like it."

The tall, brooding Guardian looked at Marcy for a moment, challenging her silently. She looked away first. He made her uneasy but not because he brought an element of danger with him. More because she had to fight the urge to stare at him.

Marcy turned her attention to the trainees and hoped they couldn't make out her blush. "We're only allowed to enter six different parts on earth. The Americas being three of the six. That limits our selection, especially since there are countless other Shadow trainees with their groups dream weaving in the same locations."

"What about Florida?" someone murmured.

"We were told western seaboard. We will do what needs to be done." She tried not to act exasperated, and instead, grabbed her small shoulder pack and threw it on.

"Um, I have a question," Mathilde raised her hand.

Marcy's anger slowly diffused as she took a deep breath. She couldn't be upset at Mathilde. She heard from Guardians that love was a human ailment, a weakness that Shadows should leave alone, but since Shadows were descendants of humans from long ago, it was a weakness they all struggled with. Just like the longing to belong. Shadows were close with each other, especially to those they grew up with. Marcy, however, never saw love or even friendship as a weakness. She longed for the closeness of a human family, and Mathilde was the closest to her heart. "What?" she asked a bit gentler this time.

"This might not be a good time to ask this, but can I please have humans above the age of ten? Unicorns and ninja turtles can drive a Shadow mad."

A pause hung in the air as each trainee stared at Mathilde like she had lost her mind. Then the snickering started.

Another young trainee added, "Amen to that!"

Even Marcy started to laugh. The laughter rose in waves until Marcy had to hold her sides. Mathilde only looked around in bewilderment saying, "What? I don't get it. What's so funny?" This didn't make the situation any better. Only Mathilde and the

Guardian stood perplexed.

Once Marcy controlled her laughter, she said, "Ancient laws dictate that younger trainees dream-weave children," then stopped herself. "Oh, who cares? It's your call."

The cheers went up and Marcy found herself smiling. Until the Guardian stepped forward. Even though he didn't have Lynde's height and weight, he still stood over the trainees. "Ancient laws are not broken. Ever. Sorry, kid. You're stuck with unicorns and…ninja turtles."

The laughter dissipated quickly, and the trainees observed him with more trepidation. He didn't act nearly as angry or monstrous as the last Guardian apprentice. Instead, he was sarcastic and condescending. Marcy didn't know which one was worse.

He extended his arm, and a curtain of blue mist descended over them, and it flowed around them. It shimmered and glowed; it pulled at the trainees who took tentative steps toward it.

The trainees "oohed." Marcy rolled her eyes in annoyance. That's all this guy needed.

"Yep, that's right, kids," he said bored. "I have a bigger blue mist. Amazing."

"Come on," she said to the trainees and walked through without looking at him.

"I have never said this before, and will deny it if anyone asks, but I have never been attracted to a Guardian until now. That Guardian is better looking than anything! Spirit or mortal," Tiya, a trainee Marcy's age, commented under her breath.

"I hate unicorns and ninja turtles." Mathilde came up behind Marcy and whispered in her ear.

Marcy laughed again, "There're thousands of dreams you can weave."

"You know what I mean," Mathilde sighed.

"Trust me, some of the stuff in adult memories is worse. Far worse."

"Yeah, some of the children have sad memories too."

"Do what you can to give them happy or peaceful dreams," Marcy interrupted.

"Why would human adults be so evil?" Mathilde continued. "It makes me want to retaliate."

They stood hand in hand observing the crashing waves of the Pacific Ocean off the Washington coast.

"I know," Marcy finally admitted. "Some humans are dark. Those are the ones I leave alone."

"If you had the power to do something, would you?" she asked.

Marcy watched each wave fall into itself. She didn't know how to answer. She didn't want to admit to feeling powerless pretty much all the time. She only felt relief from the despair when she dream-weaved. When she put what little power she had to good use. There may have been times she weaved crazy dreams, but it was just for fun. But those were harmless. Most of the time she brought thoughts of peace and tranquility, diffused anger, and strengthened confidence. She tried. But was it enough?

Marcy glanced around and noticed the other trainees standing near each other reveling in the view. Human pedestrians walked past most of them on occasion, but being dematerialized meant that a Shadow wasn't seen. Many of the humans walked holding hands. A family passed by at one point; the father hoisting his daughter over his shoulders, the mother chasing the little boy. She turned back to the churning ocean and closed her eyes. Marcy didn't know how evil existed in such a place of beauty, but she didn't want anything to do with that darkness.

The trainees stayed quiet for some time. It was extremely rare to encounter an awake human. Marcy experienced them quite a bit, but not the others. One of them said, "It would be nice to have a family, wouldn't it?"

"Don't you have dreams to weave?" The Guardian stood behind her. "There are rows of condominiums around us. Get these trainees working."

"They're not asleep yet," Marcy muttered. "It's not even ten o'clock in mortal hours." Then ignoring the Guardian, she said to the others, "Check out those stars. You don't see stars like that every night."

She and the others looked up and marveled at the beauty of the night sky. Suddenly, a tall blue mist hung in front of the view. Marcy whipped her head around to see the Guardian's hand extended and annoyance on his face.

"Do you mind?" she shot out. She needed to be careful, but her despair and jealousy at the human families and this beautiful universe they lived in led way to the anger. "Can't we at least enjoy the view until the mortals settle down for the night?"

"We are not here to enjoy the mortal realm. So, are you going to do your job, or am I going to force you through that mist, which by the way, will take you somewhere you would never want to go? But what is not an option," he said, and his eyes turned red hot and into thin slits, "is for you to ignore me."

Arec pulled at her arm. "Come on," he said low. "Let's get moving. Unless you want to try and pull what you did last night."

The Guardian, obviously overhearing Arec, smirked. "She will follow orders and dream weave. She will not *pull* what she did last night. Not if she wants to see another starlit sky."

Marcy wanted nothing more than to throw this arrogant Guardian on his backside, but she wasn't sure she could even do that again. Maybe it had been a fluke, but she didn't want to take the risk again of becoming a pile of ash. So, she swallowed back her pride, and stormed away, making sure to *accidentally* shove him. Bad move. As soon as her shoulder touched his arm, an explosion of heat threw her as she sailed onto the ground face first.

The trainees seemed to be holding back laughter, as she got on her knees and spat out the dirt and pebbles that had found a place in her mouth. She swiped at her face and clothes and holding her head high, stood up and faced the kids. They were *really* trying not to laugh. The Guardian observed her humorously as well. "Any other stupid move you want to try?"

Marcy glared at him with such intensity that the Guardian actually blinked and glanced away. He ordered the others to work.

Marcy kept staring at him because it felt as if he was hiding his discomfort. He wouldn't look at her, instead, he faced the ocean. "You have a job to do," he said in clipped words. "So, stop acting like a spoiled child and do your job."

"I hate you," she said to him. "And I hate everything about our realm. Hell sucks."

The Guardian's eyebrows raised still not facing her. "So? Do you think anyone cares about a Shadow slave? I mean, call yourself a trainee if it makes you feel better, but you are all nothing more than slaves. Trust me, it only gets worse from here. Now go."

Heat flushed her cheeks. Still, she stuck her chin out. "You're a monster. All Guardians are. Evil, conniving monsters whose only purpose for existence is to be hated by all."

For a brief second, Marcy thought she saw the Guardian's countenance falter, but no. It was still stone. "Be careful," he said quietly.

She stepped into a shadow. "Mathilde, let's go."

Blindly, she shifted from shadow to shadow, creating as much distance as possible from that Guardian.

"Wait!" she heard Mathilde call out. "You're moving too fast."

Marcy stopped and stepped out of a shadow, deciding to materialize. The mortal realm seemed so much easier. Humans may have been complex, but their memories were intriguing, and Marcy longed for their experiences. Where they didn't have to worry about stupid Guardians and joining the ranks.

"Marcy!" Mathilde gasped. "What are you doing?"

Marcy ignored her, stepped back into a shadow, and started moving from one shadow to another. In that instant, the fear had disappeared, and a stubborn fury had taken its place. Death was better than continuing to be a slave for eternity. "I'm not stopping here. Let's keep moving."

"Where are we going?" one of the other girls asked as they all endeavored to keep up.

Marcy felt her jaw clench in complete defiance. "To get a burger."

7

Different

Tor stepped through the mist to Drakkon's throne room. It was empty. "Drakkon!" he called out.

Drakkon entered the room through his own mist, leaving one of the torture chambers. The screams of the afflicted followed him. "What are you doing here? Aren't you supposed to be with the Shadow slaves?"

"They'll be fine."

"You left them unattended?"

"What is going on?" Tor demanded. "Who is she? And what kind of power does she have?"

"Is that not why I put you with her? To discover who or what she is? And yet, here you are."

"She's different," Tor explained.

"I know. I told you that."

Tor's insides still buzzed from whatever electrical current she possessed. "And I sense that you know more than you are sharing. I demand to know who she is and where she came from!"

Drakkon stepped forward and said, "Careful, Tor. I take orders from no one."

"She's different," Tor repeated, keeping the edge of the words in check. "I would like to know what I'm dealing with."

"Lynde!" Drakkon called the name loudly. He said it one more time, then sat on his throne and waited.

Lynde eventually stepped through his mist and entered. "You called? I'm overseeing some Shadow trainees."

"What can you tell us about this girl from last night?"

"I'm not sure what happened last night, but it won't happen again."

"What did happen? I'm trying to find answers. A little help would be great." Drakkon's words sounded friendly, but his tight smile and cold gaze indicated his lack of patience.

"She has blue eyes, and when I tried to punish her for insubordination, she somehow pushed me away from her."

Drakkon said nothing. He merely watched Lynde then Tor, lifting one eyebrow.

"She's not from here. From hell." As Tor said the words, he felt the slight shift in atmosphere. It had come from Lynde. He turned and studied the large guardian. He knew something. But if he knew something, why hadn't he said anything? The thought came quickly, startling him, *He's protecting her*. He cast the thought aside. Guardians don't protect Shadows, especially trainees. They break them into servitude. Just the same, this Lynde was hiding something.

"Then how do you explain how she got here?" Drakkon's voice brought Tor from his thoughts.

"I've trained in every level of this place, and nothing here is like her. Not even the human souls who reside in the lake of fire." He thought about telling Drakkon more, but he didn't want to reveal weakness. And Drakkon would see Tor's internal reactions to her as weakness. He might even tie Tor up and order the girl to stare at him until he imploded.

"May I suggest a course of action?" Lynde interrupted Tor's thoughts.

Drakkon motioned with his hand to continue.

"This Shadow trainee refuses to follow orders. It is time we move her from trainee to indentured slave. Take some of that independence from her."

"Yes, I see your point, but what if she has some sort of ability that I can use?"

"What better way than to join the ranks? You have much more interactions with those Shadows once they join."

Drakkon frowned in disgust. "And even that is too much interaction. What a sorry lot those Shadows are. If it wasn't for their ability to manipulate mortal minds, I'd destroy them all."

"Let Tor try his hand at killing her," Lynde said. "If she dies, well, she is not as powerful as we thought. If she lives through Tor's attacks, we might see what abilities she may be hiding."

"If she lives through my attack?" Tor scoffed at Lynde. "She doesn't stand a chance."

"I thought the same thing too."

"Enough." Drakkon got up and approached them. "This is ridiculous. She's a pathetic Shadow trainee. If for some reason she is an anomaly, then we'll deal with it."

"So, kill her?" A part of Tor revolted at the thought of hurting her, but he mentally shook himself. He had no time for compassion or any other human weakness.

"I told you earlier to see what kind of power she has, if any, and to kill her if she becomes a nuisance. Were those directions not clear?"

Tor caught Drakkon's sarcasm. "They were clear."

"Then why I am standing here talking to you?"

Why *had* Tor called for him? Because he had never experienced anything like it. This young woman…this pathetic Shadow trainee…had a type of power that could defeat Tor. He doubted she knew it, or he would have already been dead. Without answering, Tor extended his arm, created a mist to take him back to the western seaboard, and stepped through it.

There was only one thing to do. Take no chances. Kill her before she could kill him.

8

No Mercy

The girls picked up the whole crew of trainees. Each stayed in shadows in a secluded wooded area, other than Marcy, who stepped out and into view. "I shouldn't have told you," Mathilde whispered from a nearby shadow.

"Told me what?" Marcy asked.

"Told you about what I heard. Now you're acting all crazy and are going to go and get yourself disintegrated, which will royally suck, by the way."

"What does it matter?" Marcy countered. "If what you heard was true, then I might as well enjoy a burger." She turned to everyone before Mathilde could say anything more. "Since we were forced here too early, we might as well live a little. Just the same, stay in the shadows. I will come back outside as soon as I get the food."

"How are you going to do it?" Tiya asked. "That's a lot of burgers to stuff in your jacket."

"Let me help," Mathilde volunteered. "I will step into the cashier's shadow and alter his memory of your order."

"A senior trainee should do that," Arec said.

Everyone murmured assent.

"What is with you guys always following orders?" Marcy looked at Mathilde with a wicked grin. "Here's your chance to check out some mortal older than ten."

Any reservations Mathilde might have had previously evaporated into the early night air. "Yes!" she cheered.

"Maybe I should do it," Arec said to Marcy.

"Right," Marcy bit back the sarcasm. "Because bypassing dream weaving to go to a burger joint is definitely not breaking the rules."

Arec shrugged. "Whatever."

Marcy ran across the road, avoiding shadows. She liked the feeling of being visible for all to see. She stepped inside and inhaled the aroma of flame-broiled burgers and French fries. The cashier checked out Marcy with a knowing grin. Marcy smiled tightly then spotted Mathilde in a back shadow. In one move, she was inside the guy's head. Marcy second-guessed her decision. This human's thoughts probably weren't too pure. But the decision had been made.

"What can I do for you?"

Marcy ignored his mortal attempts at mating and ordered twelve burgers, French fries, and milkshakes.

"That's $66.57," he said with a wink.

Marcy thought quickly. What was Mathilde doing? Marcy put on the charm, "Oh no, where did I put my money?" She checked her pockets, but still, the guy said nothing.

"Do you have the money or not?"

Marcy tried to transmit her thoughts into his like the Elder Shadows could do. Nothing. Maybe she had to touch him. *Disgusting.*

The greasy guy suddenly blinked and looked at Marcy in confusion. "I'm sorry. I think you overpaid." He called back to some harried night manager who came up and keyed in a code to open up the register. He handed Marcy $61.57. "Sorry about that," he said. Then with a smirk, he added, "I can repay you even more if you want. My shift ends soon."

"It sounds tempting, but I'm really busy tonight."

Marcy juggled the bags and drinks, having to make two trips. Mathilde came around the corner, taking the last drink carrier.

Once Marcy made the second trip to the woods, the trainees hooted in excitement. They stepped out of the shadows, and devoured the meals, groaning in so much delight, that Marcy had to shush them a few times. It wasn't until she was halfway done with her own that she noticed the Guardian standing at the edge of the tree line, his eyes no longer an annoyed orange. They had full flames.

"The Guardian found us," someone said.

Marcy's heart pounded, but she acted oblivious to him.

The Guardian glowed with a reddish aura, flames exploding from his hands and head. And he was staring right at her.

"We've got to go," she whispered, picking up the leftover fast-food containers.

Everyone stayed silent as they made their way over to him. A few whimpered in fear. Marcy felt immediate remorse that she had caused this and hoped that the Guardian would only punish her.

He raised one hand and pointed flames in Marcy's direction. "The rest of you have one second to do your job before you're nothing but a pile of ash."

Marcy felt a sliver of relief. But only for a moment. This Guardian didn't act like others who scared the trainees with fury. This one emanated power, like one flick of his hand could turn the earth on its axis.

The trainees slipped into shadows, but Mathilde hung back. "What about Marcy?"

"Go," Marcy told her. "I'll be fine."

The Guardian didn't respond.

Mathilde hesitated.

"*Go*," Marcy said.

Mathilde stepped into a shadow and was gone.

Marcy glared at the Guardian, and for a brief moment, his flames dimmed. But it was too brief. He immediately growled and shot flames from his entire person. "I have a job to do," she said and tried to step into a shadow.

In the blink of an eye, he materialized beside her and grabbed her arm. She could feel the heat from his breath, but more importantly, she could feel the fire from his touch course through her veins.

And not the good kind of fire.

Marcy sucked in a breath; her lips quivering in pain.

"Follow me," he ordered and strengthened his hold. "Unless you want your little slaves to watch you die. You know as well as I do, they are lurking close by."

Marcy nodded before her insides were singed into smithereens. He released her, and she fell to the ground. She took in a few shaky breaths but refused to look up at him. Shame and humiliation hurt almost as much as his touch. He was no regular Guardian; that much she was sure on. He contained too much power but so had Lynde. How had she pushed him off?

She didn't feel him near her anymore, and she also felt the cool sensation that she had felt when Lynde had tried to extinguish her. She did not relish going through that again. "Think, Marcy. Think," she whispered. What she needed was time. She needed to figure out what happened with the other Guardian and practice whatever skill she possessed. Taking a quick glance beside her, Marcy saw her escape. If she could only step into that shadow, she could get away.

Anything was better than following this Guardian to a—no doubt—secure location where she would probably be killed.

No, she had to try. Maybe she could lose him and hide somewhere while she figured out a plan.

She glanced up.

The woods. He was going to drag her deep into the woods. Probably cause a forest fire. Not that Guardians cared. She had heard how they sometimes started fires to rile the humans up.

Marcy slowly stood up, the cooling sensation still coursed

through her, and it seemed to give her strength. She looked over at him, met his gaze, and acted like she was about to move toward him. In less than a second, she stepped into a shadow and dematerialized. This time she moved before he did. She made sure to shift in as random a pattern as she could. The problem was she was so nervous, she hadn't kept tabs on where she was heading. She glanced behind herself to see if she was being followed.

And hit something hard.

Marcy flew through the air. She slammed against the ground and immediately felt the broken bones. She screamed in pain, jerking her head back and forth, since that's the only thing that could move.

The Guardian towered over her, flames billowing from him.

Marcy bit her lip, forcing herself not to beg for mercy. Besides, as she evened her breathing, the cooling balm seemed to liquefy her insides. She didn't want to give that away. If he didn't know about it, she wondered if she could use the element of surprise to her advantage. She'd experienced this sensation enough to figure out that somehow it acted as a healing agent. This might be—yet again—something that differentiated her from the crowd, but this time, she welcomed the difference. Especially if would keep her alive.

He knelt beside her; his flame dimmed. He almost looked guilty. Emotion sucker-punched Marcy. His face looked human. Like he was sad.

"How'd you do it?" she whispered, still in pain. "How did you get ahead of me?"

He searched her face before answering, "I can move much faster than you. It's not necessarily a Guardian thing. It's more like a *me* thing. What about you? How do you do it?"

"Do what?" Suddenly, she yelped as a bone snapped into place. She pushed herself back and gritted her teeth as a rib pushed into its correct position. Marcy hated giving the Guardian the satisfaction of seeing her agony.

He created a fireball. "Never mind. It doesn't matter."

Another rib snapped into place. Marcy yelled in pain. The cooling agent worked fast, but not fast enough. She forced herself to even out her breathing as a tear escaped.

"I don't know what I was worried about," he said to himself. "When push comes to shove, you are still nothing but a Shadow."

"Kill me," Marcy said. "Do it. I would rather die than be a slave for eternity."

"Wish granted." The fire was immediate. Marcy screamed in pain, opening her eyes in shock and desperation. His eyes and aura exploded in flames. This wasn't gradual, like with Lynde. This was a fireball deep inside. The excruciating pain stopped her breath.

Betraying herself, she croaked out, "Mercy."

The Guardian brought her face close to his and with his lips barely touching hers, said, "No." He breathed a deathly flame that traveled to her heart.

Marcy's eyes rolled to the back of her head. The last thing she remembered before dying was the flame exploding inside her.

9

It's Finished

Something wasn't right.

She hadn't disintegrated. Tor stepped back, shocked at the sight before him. The girl, Marcy, lay dead, nothing but a charred corpse. But she should have turned to ash. There should be nothing left. He had given it everything he had.

"She's dead," he said to himself. "That's what matters." But he could not stop the feeling that something was very wrong. Then he remembered Lynde. The other Guardian knew something. Tor needed to find out. Especially with the thought that nagged him: what if he had just killed the one who could have ended his torture? "Stop it," he ordered himself. But it was the mortal realm. He couldn't stay for long without feeling its effects.

Taking one last look, he left the charred body in the woods and materialized at the oceanfront where the other trainees would be waiting. He doubted they did any dream weaving. Just another Shadow weakness. Caring for others.

He sensed their presence, as he had in the woods. They had seen their fellow trainee die. "No dream weaving. I've accomplished what I set out to do. Let's go." He extended the blue mist and waited.

One by one, the trainees stepped out of the shadows and walked through the mist. No one spoke to him. No one so much as looked at him. The heaviness of grief sat upon their shoulders, and for a moment, he felt guilty. But only for a moment. "Stupid human emotions," he muttered, as he walked through the blue mist, leaving the mortal realm and its side effects behind.

10

Unfinished Business

Marcy squinted until she adjusted to the light. She didn't know the room she was standing in but recognized it as some type of medical facility. There was little décor on the walls, but there was a lot of equipment. It was eerily quiet. She walked out of the room and nearly collided with a woman in a wheelchair, a frantic man pushing her inside, and a nurse saying, "This room here."

Marcy ducked back into the room, intrigued and perplexed at the scene in front of her.

The woman panted, holding her enlarged belly. The man had a scruffy beard but kind eyes, and he murmured things in the woman's ear. The pregnant woman's hair was plastered to her head with sweat. The nurse attached devices and moved different medical instruments in place.

"Just keep breathing rhythmically," the nurse said with a strong Irish accent.

"Drugs," the young woman said. "Please. Something."

The nurse smiled reassuringly. "Remember, we've been working on this. You wanted a natural birth. That's why you hired me as your midwife. Besides you're already dilated to eight and doing fantastic."

The woman responded by arching her back and moaning. The man held her hand as she squeezed it.

Marcy cringed at the woman's pain. She couldn't have been older than her early twenties. Something nagged at her, something she should know.

"It'll be soon," the midwife said.

The woman's agony tore at Marcy. Something was pulling inside her. This place was familiar.

As the woman pushed and screamed and the midwife assisted, Marcy had to look away. When she did, her blood stopped cold.

She had heard of horrendous demons personifying evil, but she had lived a relatively tame existence and never encountered one. Now she had to swallow back bile.

It wasn't just his appearance, even though it was grotesque and nerve-wracking, but it was the hate his aura pushed off as he watched the birth. He looked ready to kill. Not just kill but maybe eat everyone in the room.

For some reason, he didn't see Marcy standing there. She heard the wails of the newborn but couldn't take her eyes off the demon. She felt a fierce protection for this family and would stop this demon, or at least try.

Then Kraal stepped out of the shadow, and Marcy took a step back in surprise. He was young. Joining the ranks had aged him, but here, he looked not much older than Marcy.

"Kraal?" she asked, though he didn't hear.

He was talking to the demon, but she couldn't hear his words.

They were deciding something. Kraal didn't look too happy.

Marcy watched as he shifted from one human to the other. Then her gaze fell on the child, and she was mesmerized. She took tentative steps and reached out, wanting to hold the infant. The mother sang, and Marcy's world stopped for a moment.

"The song," she whispered.

But then it was darkness, and all she heard was her own voice, humming the tune.

The first thing Marcy noticed when she became semi-coherent was the dryness of her mouth. Her eyes were gritty and hurt to open them.

The dream lingered, but she didn't know what to make of any of it. Not only because she had never had a full dream before, but mostly because her insides were fried.

She coughed violently, vomiting soot and ash, the charcoal taste stinging as it forced its way out. Marcy clutched her stomach, the burning sensation not quite ebbed.

As she panted out breaths, she felt a light breeze on her face. She was still in the mortal realm. Everything came back sharply. The clarity as clear as glass. The Guardian had killed her. She had felt her insides burst. Yet, whatever he had meant to do, didn't happen, because Marcy felt very much alive.

Why were Guardians such monsters? He was cold and calculating and a murderer. Well, she wasn't dead—which brought her a bit of smugness—but he was at the very least an attempted murderer.

The cooling agent kept running through her body in waves, each time helping her breathe a little better. Whatever was going on with her, she was glad her body had this device to heal.

Eventually, she could sit up. She hugged her knees; the breeze helped bring relief to the stuffiness she felt inside. Strong cramps started inside her like a steel clamp twisting her insides. Each cramp seemed to intensify. She gritted her teeth and fought back the urge to cry out in pain. Then, something bizarre started happening. With each painful twist, a powerful energy surged through her fingertips. With the surge came an intense vibration that traveled so violently through her body that she had to lay back down again.

Maybe the Guardian did this. Maybe she would die in phases. The vibrations seized her body, shaking her from head to toe.

What did he do? She could barely think coherently. This was torture. A slow, painful death? Why couldn't he have made it quick?

She screamed now, clawing at the ground. Turning over, she vomited again.

Then as quickly as it came, the vibrations and cramping subsided.

Marcy needed water. Her mouth tasted like the remnants of a finished fire, and her throat was so closed up, she could barely swallow. Getting her bearings, she stumbled to her knees, then to her feet. The sensation inside still vibrated but more to the rhythm of her heart. Every part of her seemed to thrum. But none of that mattered. She needed water.

It didn't take Marcy long to realize she was in the same woods as before. He had left her there.

She told herself to contain her fury. The time would come for her to exact vengeance. The key, for right now, was survival. So, when she stumbled out of the woods, she spotted the burger joint from before. That seemed long ago. It was dark, but Marcy doubted it was the same night. The wind was strong. It would rain soon.

How did Marcy know that? She *felt* it.

The energy seemed to open up all these parts to her. Like she sensed the nearest person was driving in a car and would pass her in less the two minutes.

She didn't even think about it. Just stepped into a shadow and stepped back out into the restaurant. There she was, at the soda machine, pressing the water button, leaning down with her head back, and guzzling the liquid in hungry gulps.

The water brought immediate relief. After several minutes of satisfying her thirst, Marcy stood back up, combed her fingers through her hair, and then brought her hair to her nose.

Great. No more fruity scent.

She sat down with another cup of water and thought about each event. So, Drakkon was trying to kill her. Marcy didn't think it was just because she was rebellious. There had to be something more. It had to do with whatever powers were contained inside of her.

She *should* have died. Shadows don't recover from a Guardian's disintegrating attack. But now, not only had she lived, but he seemed to have awakened something in her. Something itching to get out.

But she shoved all that aside and thought about the dream. Those had to be her parents. She knew it. And that baby was her. The demon was there to kill the baby. Kraal, too?

She couldn't think about the betrayal; first, she had to put together the pieces to the puzzle.

They obviously wanted her dead at birth. Why? And why did they let her live, only to try to kill her again?

Maybe they didn't let *you live*, she thought. *Maybe they couldn't kill you.*

Whatever the case may be, Marcy realized that somewhere she had parents. Human parents. Parents who no longer had a daughter.

Marcy stood up quickly. "I'm going to find them," she whispered. It made sense. She didn't fit in Levea. She looked human because she was human. She had no clue why she could dream weave and not die when demons and Guardians tried to kill her. No wonder she felt the earth was where she belonged!

Since Drakkon and everyone thought she was dead, they wouldn't be looking for her. She thought of Mathilde and the other Shadow trainees, and even though she longed to hug her and at least tell her goodbye, she wouldn't be able to rest until she found the man and woman who had given her life. Maybe they would know who or what she was.

Stepping into a shadow, she stepped out onto the pavement. So, where did she start?

Computers held databases. She'd seen them before, and humans had multiple memories about them. A library. Yes, that's where a computer would be. Where else? A store. Marcy had seen them at stores. Still, she wondered if she should investigate a few humans' memories to see if she could discover some more information.

She started shifting through shadows to the suburbs she had seen earlier. It was the darkest part of the night. Shadows would already be done. But she'd have to be careful.

Once out of a shadow, she checked out the houses and picked an end one that had a few cars. There had to be someone in there with memories of computers.

Before she moved, her hair raised on the back of her neck. Something was moving. A lot of somethings. A cold sensation trickled through her veins. She stepped back into a shadow beside a car and crouched, just in case whatever it was could see the spirit realm.

Nothing. Everything seemed still.

Marcy went to step out of the shadow when she heard the chattering. High-pitched, distinctive language. It was everywhere. She couldn't shake the cold, menacing feeling.

Marcy wondered if she should take off. It was definitely evil, and after seeing the hideous demon in the dream, she didn't want to know what else was out there. Shadow trainees were protected for a reason. Yet, Marcy also knew that if she wanted to know the truth, she needed to know what was out there. She needed to figure out what was truly going on. She began to believe, especially after that vivid dream, that there was a larger picture she wasn't privy to.

The chattering grew in volume and numbers. Marcy studied the scene and at first didn't notice anything unusual. Then movement caught her eye. A little creature jumped from a porch to a window sill to a second-floor window, laughing and chattering. The creature walked upright, but couldn't have been bigger than a human infant. It didn't have any features; it was just a black mass outlining a somewhat little human form.

But it could jump wherever it wanted. Now that Marcy had spotted the one, she saw the dark creatures everywhere, jumping from one house to another. One window had a pile of them pushing to get in. A light in the bedroom turned on, and before Marcy could blink, they scattered into the darkness.

They were from the spiritual realm, but what were they? How many other creatures were out there? She remembered the demon in the dream and shuddered. Was this the side she was on? And who was their enemy? And if all these creatures seemed so dark and sinister, what was the other side like?

Swallowing any fear, she reached out her hand toward a rock the size of her palm. It was just out of reach. She stretched until her fingers almost touched it. A tingling sensation increased at her fingertips until the rock flew into her hand.

Marcy stared at it in shock. Did she just do that?

She set the rock down and tried again. It didn't move. She scrunched her eyebrows together and concentrated. The tingling started, but nothing happened.

Exhaling, she picked it up.

The clump of creatures pushed themselves into another window, their chatter so high-pitched, that Marcy wanted to cover her ears.

One flew out from behind the car and jumped onto another window, but not without giving Marcy a minor heart attack.

A dog barked across the street from where she crouched hidden. Could the dog see?

The chatter became faster—if that was possible—and one after another jumped on the dog until he was covered by a black, moving mass. The dog whimpered, and Marcy's heart tugged. Before she knew what she was doing, she threw the rock at the mass of creatures. She was too far to hit them, but the tingling surged through her and the rock sailed across the street, hitting the edge of the mass with a ting.

Their heads collectively turned toward her, and not just the one clump. All the creatures in her eyesight jumped off the houses in unison, coming together in the middle of the street. The chatter seemed to be a definite language, but she couldn't understand it. All she knew was that dematerialized or not, these creatures could see her.

"Stupid move," she muttered. At least the dog had taken off into his doghouse.

Marcy thought of options. If she fled, would they follow? They had tremendous movement already. Still, even if she wanted to move, she couldn't. She couldn't take her eyes off the creatures as they converged together into one mass. The mass grew and expanded, and still, Marcy could not move. The mass moved toward her.

Instinctively, she stood up to face it. Her hands tingled with whatever was inside her.

By the time they reached her, they had formed a tall form of a human figure, completely disguised in black. Marcy could only make out the outlines of the eyes and mouth. The chattering, however, sounded like a collective group.

The eyes—or the outline of them—bore into Marcy, as if trying to read her. The chattering intensified to such a fever that she covered her ears. Her insides began to hum as the tingling sensation worked to her fingertips. She didn't think about it, she only stuck her hands forward and hit the creature with as much force as she could. "Quiet!"

The mass flew back as the creatures were thrown everywhere.

This time she shifted as fast as she could away from the scene.

Marcy tried not to think, only to move. She stopped briefly at the ocean boardwalk desperately hoping someone had waited for her and would help. Taking a quick look around, she swallowed a bit of panic. Too much was happening to her, and she needed someone to help or explain things.

A loud, piercing scream descended from the air, and the black mass threw itself on her, exploding into smaller creatures. The crawling began all over her skin. The creatures had morphed into black cockroaches, and they were all over Marcy.

Now she screamed, knocking them off, only to have them jump right back on. She ran into a shadow, but they kept crawling.

They tried to crawl into her ears, up her nose, down her pants. No matter how she moved or how many she flung off, they were on her. Desperate, she ran into the ocean and plunged in. The cold enveloped her, but at least the crawling had stopped. She heard the chattering again. When she snuck a peek by sticking her head out of the water, they morphed into their small midget shapes, chattering angrily at each other.

But the water was like knives against her skin. Her teeth couldn't stop chattering, and her limbs were going numb. She had never been immersed in water before. She didn't like it being so cold, and she couldn't swim. A good distance away, she spotted a collection of jagged rocks sticking out of the water, but she'd have to try to swim to it. Marcy didn't know where to start. In human memories, they flapped their arms and legs a lot in the water.

Maybe she should try it. She needed to do something before she turned to a block of ice.

Death by cockroaches, or death by hypothermia?

"If I live, I'm learning to swim," Marcy said. She didn't see any other option, so she slugged through the water, entirely shaking. She could barely think. "Can we talk?" she tried.

But the creatures weren't interested in chit-chat because as she approached, they morphed into the cockroaches again, circling each other waiting to feast. What would happen if she just fell and let the nasty spirit bugs take over?

Even with the cold shakes, her instincts told her it wouldn't be a pleasant fate.

A sick feeling twisted inside, but Marcy had no other options. She tried using the power in her hands to shove them away again, but she shook too violently to hold them steady.

She stepped onto the beach and braced herself for the onslaught. The cockroaches swarmed her but only briefly before forming into the veiled image of a man. The chattering quieted, and the mouth said in clipped words, "Who sent you?"

Marcy shook her head, teeth still chattering, "No one. I only wanted to know what spirit species you are."

"Liar!" they hissed together, even though only the mouth moved. "You bare the mark of invincibility. The mark that only comes from the Nameless One."

Marcy might have been freezing to death, but she was still perplexed by what the creature said. "I don't know what mark you are talking about?"

"Invincibility mark!" it hissed louder. A cockroach fell from the image and crawled to her wrist.

She shrieked, flinging it off. But on the inside of her right wrist, she noticed what would be a human birthmark. It was shaped like a teardrop and rose slightly from the skin. But her hands shook too much for her to contemplate it for long. Marcy needed to find warmth, but how to ditch the bugs? "I need…" her teeth chattered, "warmth."

The creature let out a shriek that sent chills through Marcy. The man shifted into all the little midget creatures, and they took off in one big mass toward wherever they were going.

Marcy nearly fell over. Instead, she shivered into a shadow and shifted sporadically until she found some beachside homes. She could see more of the dark creatures around here, as well, jumping in and out of windows, but she wasn't about to draw attention to herself again.

When she found a beach house that sat dark, she paused and noticed the creatures left this house alone. It had to be uninhabited. She found enough strength to shift inside one of the shadows.

She shifted quickly through the rooms. It was empty. She stumbled into a bedroom, stripped off the wet clothes, found a blanket, wrapped herself in it, and shivered into oblivion.

11

Surprise Visitor

The nightmare was warped like looking through a distorted mirror at a cheap carnival. The woman's blood-chilling scream echoed, and Marcy knew she had to help. She ran toward the scream, in and out of corridors, through doors that only led to another one. She stopped, panting.

The wretched scream pulled at her again. This time she ran through Levea. The Shadow trainees all stopped and stared at her as if she was an intruder. She ran through tents, searching, but the scream didn't stop, and Marcy wasn't anywhere close.

"Make it stop!" she shouted, but no one was there.

She stumbled and fell. When she lifted her face, she was back in the same hospital room as before. The young woman sat on the ground, her hands covering her face. The man with the scruffy beard held his arms around her.

"What?" Marcy asked them. "What's wrong?"

The woman stopped screaming long enough to look at Marcy. She wiped away her tears and flung her arms around Marcy's neck. "There you are," she whimpered. "I thought I lost you."

When Marcy woke up, she noticed three things. She was no longer shivering, she stank something atrocious, and her stomach growled. But she didn't move. Instead, she replayed the dream in her head. The way the woman's arms felt around Marcy.

They had to be her parents! Which meant what? She had been kidnapped. By Kraal? It had to be him. Why? Why would he take a human baby from her parents?

Marcy couldn't figure out how she could be a human and a Shadow. Then again, she also had some type of invincibility mark and her fingers could tingle, so hey, who knew what the heck kind of species she was?

When she sat up, she found herself on one of the bedroom floors. She put the blanket back but felt bad for the owners. She didn't want to be someone who would stink up their blanket.

"Maybe they have detergent," she said. Leaving it for the time being, she found the attached bathroom. She exhaled in relief just looking at the size of the oversized bathtub. The owner even had an arrangement of bubble baths and salts to choose from. "Jackpot."

After a mixture of bubble baths was poured in, she turned on the faucet. The water rushed out. She went out, grabbed the blanket, and shifted until she found the laundry room. "They must be coming back," she said while looking at a fully stocked shelf of detergent, fabric softener, and dryer sheets. She threw the blanket in the washer, then went back to the bedroom for her clothes and stuffed them in the washer, too.

Once the washer was going, she shifted into the kitchen. The groceries were pretty sparse. She found an apple left in the bottom of a refrigerator tray. She grabbed it, then searched the cupboard. A jar of peanut butter would be just fine. With a spoon in hand, along with the peanut butter and apple, she stepped into a shadow and shifted back to the bathroom in under three seconds.

"Ahh," she sighed, as she sank into the water. "Perfect." The bubbles wrapped around her, and she leaned back with a smile on her face. She ate the apple, then enjoyed a couple of spoonfuls of peanut butter. Even though she was as relaxed as she had been in a while, her mind still worked in overdrive. Shadows don't dream. Yet, she could. Did someone know she could dream? Could someone be manipulating her dreams?

She doubted it. The dreams seemed real. They were about the same couple, and she didn't start having them until after the first Guardian nearly killed her.

Marcy took a washcloth and began scrubbing her legs and arms. She wished she had someone to talk to, but she felt more like an outsider than ever before. Would she be in the mortal realm forever? It's what she wanted, wasn't it? What she thought she had wanted didn't seem so perfect without her friends.

And this last Guardian. What was his name? *Tor.*

Her blood began to boil when she thought about him. Oh, she wanted to see him again and torture him. Even if it wasn't possible, she'd still have fun trying. Marcy wondered if her powers were working. She reached her hand up toward a shampoo bottle and focused. The tingle was there.

"Come on," she whispered.

She felt a shot of electricity course through her as the shampoo bottle sailed right into her hand. Staring at it in wonder, she whispered, "Cool."

As she poured shampoo into her palm, she noticed the birthmark on her wrist. She'd seen it before but never had thought about it. Mark of invincibility?

Marcy sunk under the water and scrubbed and rinsed her hair. She was determined to find answers. How? She had no idea.

When she came back up, she wiped the bubbles from her face and out of her eyes. When she opened her eyes, she found a huge man with a hungry look on his face standing over her.

Marcy did the only thing she thought to do: she screamed.

"Get up," he said in the same clipped voice as the other creatures.

She stayed frozen in fear. Despite a face lined with tattoos and cut marks, his eyes were black orbs like a Shadow, but Marcy could see human souls in them trying to get out. She could hear them, too.

Marcy whimpered. He kept watching her hungrily. Bringing up one of his pointed nails, he traced it down her cheek. "Get up before I slice this pretty little face of yours."

As modestly as she could—one arm over her breasts, the other over her nether regions—she stood, her knees knocking together. She saw him lick his lips, and the apple and peanut butter nearly came back up. Tears ran down her cheeks but couldn't help it. Any confidence she had felt earlier—which wasn't much—deteriorated.

"Step out of the bathtub, little girl."

She did. He skimmed his pointed nail down her face to her neck.

Stop it! The energy in her pulsed as he dropped his hand. He laughed evilly. Still, it gave her enough time to wrap a towel around herself.

The energy was percolating deep within.

"The towel's not going to protect you." He stood so close, that the souls in his eyes wailed at her.

Furious, she closed her eyes and summoned all her power into throwing him off. Her hand seemed to move on its own as the energy poured out of her in a flash. It threw him into the hall.

But the force didn't knock him down, and he now looked furious. "Is that all you've got," he smirked and marched into the bathroom. He grabbed her hair and smacked her against the wall. She saw stars. When she tried to move, she realized she couldn't. He had some force that he was using to keep her in place.

"Please," she started. "I can explain. The Guardian tried to kill me, but I didn't do anything wrong. If I could speak to Drakkon, I can explain." She trembled with fury but stayed completely paralyzed.

"Say goodbye," he whispered menacingly. "Here is where I take your soul."

Marcy's fury mixed with the energy inside of her and bubbled up until she screamed with everything she had. She willed him not to touch her and squeezed her eyes shut in concentration.

When the scream died from her lips, she opened her eyes to

brace herself but found he had taken a few steps back and was watching her perplexed. What she also noticed was a fine mist blanketed her from head to toe.

The curiosity quickly ended for the monster. He tried to grab her again, but he couldn't touch the mist without getting some kind of shock.

"Drop the shield!" he roared in anger.

"Unparalyze me!" she demanded in return.

"The shield will wear off soon enough, and then I will make you beg for death."

"It stays here as long as I want it to," Marcy said, trying to sound confident.

He stood over Marcy, panting heavily, growing larger with each inhaled breath. His form morphed until what hovered over Marcy truly was a monster with sharp feathered wings and eyes that seemed to take up half the creature's face. The souls inside them yelled in terror, biting themselves and thrashing around.

Marcy was so struck with fear that the mist shifted slightly. The creature was ready and much faster, whipping his lizard-like tongue at her, wrapping it around her.

She screamed again, trying to reinforce the shield, but the creature lunged upward completely slipping through humanity's barriers. It flew at an incredible speed, taking a naked Marcy with it. Her scream seemed stuck in her throat, but probably because since it flew so fast, she couldn't breathe.

Then the atmosphere changed. She heard the waterfall before

she saw it. The creature released her as she dropped into the vast nothingness the waterfall descended into.

She hit the lush green grass with a splat, but it sucked her into it and brought her back up. Marcy lay face down and had to do a quick check to make sure she hadn't lost a limb somewhere.

Marcy lifted her head and saw the waterfall. She snuck a glance around and noticed pillars and a throne that took up most of the landscape. Marcy's gut twisted at the sight of the horrid creatures that surrounded the throne. All of which now watched her. She noticed the small black creatures from the night before, some Elder Shadows whose faces had deformed into hideous masks. They seemed heavy with sorrow and grief. Several creatures were similar to the flying monster that brought her here. The one who had brought her now appeared as the disgusting man who had tried to touch and violate her.

Marcy couldn't decide who she feared the most.

There were Guardians, as well. Two, to be exact. Lynde was there, standing ominously. The other was the one who left her in the forest. *Tor.* His face couldn't mask the shock when their eyes met. Marcy would have liked to glory in that look, but she was too busy tightening the towel around her. Thankfully, it had mostly stayed put for the journey.

Now that she was sitting, she saw the elegant man who sat on the throne. He was beautiful and such a contrast to the ugliness around him. Eyes bluer than hers. Hair so blonde it almost looked translucent. Full lips that were smiling down at her with perfect teeth.

"Hello, Marcy," he said in a melodious voice.

"Hello."

"You've seemed to find trouble lately," he said, standing up and walking to her.

"Yes."

"Tell me what happened." His invitation relaxed her somewhat, as he knelt beside her.

She gazed into the kindness of his eyes. How could he surround himself with such atrocities?

"A Guardian tried to kill me, then abandoned me in the mortal realm," she stammered.

Righteous indignation lit up in his eyes. "That's horrible."

"Then I met the little black creatures who turned into cockroaches and tried to eat me." Marcy didn't know what they had been trying to do. "And this…thing…right here," she pointed at the man-beast who had brought her, "He tried to take my soul." She shivered at the memory.

"And yet, here you are," the beautiful man said, getting up. He turned to the other creatures. "Here she is unscathed and very much alive."

His tune had changed. There was a sharpness to it. Marcy glanced up confused.

"Tor," he called out.

"Sir," the young Guardian stepped forward. There was no cockiness anymore. He appeared intimidated and anxious.

"What. Happened." His words were clipped with anger. Was he upset over what this Guardian had done? Or over what he hadn't accomplished?

The energy hummed inside Marcy, and it gave off a sense of wariness and caution. She carefully watched the beautiful man trying to fight back whatever calming technique he was using. Marcy concentrated and could faintly see shiny scales where his skin should have been. Whoever, or whatever, he was, he was powerful because she couldn't break down whatever illusion he had created.

"I did everything that was commanded of me." This time Marcy could hear an edge of defiance in his voice.

"And…?" He turned to the black creatures who chattered away in their own language.

Last, he turned to the monstrous man who still had his eyes on Marcy with a desirous look of wanting to swallow her whole. Finally, he said, "She evoked a shield."

Now the beautiful man acted surprised. So did everyone, including Tor, who couldn't seem to tear his eyes away from Marcy. Marcy was too frightened to revel in it. Then her gaze landed on Lynde who seemed to watch her with admiration. His eyes were blue again. The energy pounded in her ears. He seemed to mentally shake himself because he broke eye contact and scowled.

Marcy was drawn back to Drakkon's words. "So, you survive a master Guardian's full assault, the imps' insanity device, and a master demon's attack to steal your soul?"

"Yes?"

The imps chattered again at the man. He stopped, his face a mix of denial and irritation. Stepping over to her, he grabbed Marcy's arm and inspected the mark. He threw her arm down, swearing vehemently.

Slowly, a thought dawned on Marcy. These beings all tried to kill her. The last one brought her here. Why trust this man?

This man's power packaged itself in deception. And he was good at it.

Once the realization hit her, the illusion dropped immediately. The beautiful man was a full-fledged dragon, the color of blood with great horns, and a tail that had spikes as long as daggers.

Marcy gasped, then dropped her head before he realized his illusion no longer worked.

"What is it, dear?" he cooed in a syrupy sweet voice, which hit her ears now as an ill-played note. She even grimaced at it.

"Look at me," he commanded, any niceties gone.

Marcy looked up. The dragon stared at her, his hot breath making her cringe. In the blink of an eye, he morphed into the beautiful man again. "There. Is that better?"

"Why are you playing games with me? And why are all these *monsters* trying to kill me?" Marcy made sure to glare at the Guardian when she said the word *monsters*.

"Do you know who I am?"

"Drakkon," Marcy said simply. "But I don't know what's going on. I feel like I'm some sort of pawn, and no one is telling me anything!"

"Do you follow the rules?" he asked.

Marcy sighed in exasperation. "Are you serious? You're trying to kill me because I steal shampoo bottles?"

"When you break the rules, you put everything our armies have worked for in jeopardy. Do you want that?"

"I don't know. I don't know what we're even fighting! Shadow trainees don't exactly get told a lot."

"Feisty little thing, isn't she?" Drakkon asked his henchmen. They didn't respond, but all eyes were on her. "We're fighting a war against an enemy who has already determined that our kingdom—that means your little tent in Levea, and all your Shadow friends—is going to be taken from us."

"Why? What have we done to the Nameless One?"

Every being stopped at the title. Even Drakkon seemed to freeze in place. "Do not ever mention our great enemy in my presence." His voice sounded cold but also frightened.

A shiver ran through Marcy.

"Tor, take her back to Levea. No more mortal realm."

Marcy's jaw dropped. "Why? I won't steal anymore. I promise."

"You want me to babysit, sir?" Tor did not appear pleased at the predicament.

"Fine," Drakkon said. "Rakye, take her." The monstrous man, who turned into a demon bird and brought her here, stepped forward.

He smiled sinisterly. "I accept."

Marcy nearly whimpered.

"None of the trainees would stand a chance," Lynde said. "He'd easily destroy all of Levea."

Drakkon considered. "He's right, Rakye, you do have a problem with self-control."

"When do I get my compensation?" Rakye asked in irritation. "You said I could have her, and I'm determined to fulfill the agreement."

"Well, you had your chance, didn't you?" Drakkon responded. "Tor!"

"Sir?"

"If you disappoint me again, it will not go without punishment."

Tor nodded in understanding, but his face seemed to have a hard time containing his anger. Without looking at Marcy, he held out his hand and the blue mist appeared. "Let's go."

Marcy made sure to cover up her body with the towel as she stood.

"Oh, and Marcy?"

She turned to Drakkon. "Yes?"

"You will sign allegiance to me soon. Try to behave." His words had a foreboding edge to them.

Marcy stepped through the mist and onto the ground next to her tent. Once there, her chest started to heave as the sobs came. She ran her hands through her hair and tried to keep it together. Taking in deep breaths, she squeezed her eyes shut. *Not now*, she thought.

"You might want to get some clothes on," Tor said.

Marcy glanced up and saw Tor eyeing her.

Her hands were in her hair. She dropped them quickly and covered as best she could until she unzipped her tent and went inside.

12

Babysitting

He should have just let Rakye have her. It couldn't be sympathy. What did he care if Rakye sucked the soul right out of her? Even with the short time spent together, that Shadow chic drove him nuts. The girl was needy and annoying and emotional and...*still alive*.

If Tor wanted to be honest with himself, it was curiosity that had him agreeing to babysit. Since as far back as he could remember, he's been the one with unmatched capabilities. Not only had Drakkon himself been Tor's mentor, teaching him all the secrets of hell, but he'd trained with each demon division, learning all their tactics and how to implement them. Tor was a torture and death machine.

And he gloried in it. He knew Drakkon was grooming him to be his right-hand man. Until now. Drakkon had not been happy when Sorsa reported Marcy alone and alive in the mortal realm. Tor sighed in frustration. He should have brought her back. *Leaving her there was dumb*, he scolded himself. But he saw her dead. She had turned into a charred carcass.

Now Tor didn't know what to think. Drakkon could have taken his poisoned sword and annihilated him. Drakkon never reacted well when his plans turned out differently than his original intent. Which meant most creatures in hell feared Drakkon every moment in eternity. Since Tor was still in one piece, he reasoned that meant Drakkon couldn't be through with him yet.

If that wasn't bad enough, Rakye reported she evoked a shield. That couldn't be possible. Only the light-bearers possessed that. They were untouchable. But she couldn't be a light-bearer because their radiance could not be contained in hell.

None of it made sense. Which only frustrated Tor more.

The thought that bothered him since he saw her alive was that Drakkon might choose her instead. If she was truly powerful enough to stay alive after his death move and to survive Sorsa's insanity device and Rakye's torture, this annoying Shadow trainee could be useful when Drakkon decides to flood the earth with his fury.

So, Tor needed to watch her. See if any of this information might be true.

The girl cried from inside the tent. Tor would give it another ten seconds before he shot a fireball in there. *Human emotions.*

How ridiculous.

Tor counted in his head. 10…9…8…7…6…

His hand already held the fire ready to throw. The tent would disintegrate…the girl would be charred to ash…fire on the inside didn't work, but maybe an external flame would do the trick.

5…4…3…

Then it stopped. Tor held his breath and listened. There was a sniffle, then the girl moved swiftly, stepping out of the tent.

Tor extinguished the fireball. Bummer.

"What was that for?" she asked with enough disdain in her words to rile his anger.

"To shut you up," he said with just as much loathing.

"Mmm-hmm, like you did last time? Too bad for you it didn't work."

The tears might not have been there, but Tor sensed she put on a front. There was a sadness in her blue eyes that subdued whatever energy was within her, which he had weirdly grown to crave. But he scoffed at her anyway. "Trust me, there are ways to kill you, and we'll enjoy torturing you with every one of them."

He watched her swallow, but she kept her tough mask in place. She turned and started walking away.

"Where are you going?"

"None of your business."

"There's nowhere you can go in this place that I can't be at in less than a second, so you best answer me."

She kept walking.

Tor pressed his lips together to contain his irritation. Then he thought of where he wanted to be, took the first step, and then stood in front of the girl. She plowed into him.

"Will you stop doing that?"

"I asked where you're going, and you will answer me."

She looked up at him and met his gaze. Those eyes of hers were something. The electricity burned in him, but he refused to look away. There was something about it that felt like pure air in the lungs.

"To visit my Shadow trainee. She is probably worried, and I want her to know that I made it back…*alive.*"

Tor ignored her jab. He didn't think commiserating with her trainee would be a good thing. It might even spark hope in these pitiful Shadow trainees that any of them stand a chance of escaping Drakkon's legions. Then again, these trainees were lower than the imps, so what did it matter? They had no hope of escape. "You do not dictate what you do. Why is that hard for your brain to comprehend?"

"Drakkon said I couldn't go into the mortal realm. He didn't say anything about me having to stay in my tent."

Tor moved aside. He fell in step with her.

"How do you do that again?" she asked after a moment.

"Do what?"

"You know, go from one spot to another so quickly. Is it like shifting?"

Tor stopped the nasty comment before speaking. Drakkon might decide to use her powers, and Tor refused to be ousted. He might as well play whatever game Drakkon was playing. "I see it in my mind where I want to go. When I take the first step, I'm there."

Marcy looked fascinated despite her hatred of him. She must have caught on to her face's betrayal because her expression quickly changed. "I can do the same thing except I need a shadow."

"Then you can't do the same thing."

"Is that how you kept getting in front of me? You know, back in the mortal realm?"

Tor hid the surprise. She didn't respond to the insult. That was something he would have to watch out for. Her humanness made her unpredictable. How she could go from tears to indignation to what seemed like genuine curiosity baffled him. Not that he'd show it. But just the same, he would have to be careful.

"I'll tell you more when you tell me how you lived through my attack."

She opened her mouth to say something, but they had reached the younger trainees' tents. The young girl who had been in the mortal realm with them had already spotted her mentor.

"Marcy!" The girls embraced with genuine affection. Tor watched fascinated. He spent too much time down in the farthest reaches of hell where any sort of warm emotion simply did not exist. Drakkon hated the very idea of love or friendship unless he needed it for his advantage, and even then, it was merely a deception.

As Tor's mentor, Drakkon showed him no emotional love or support. Tor couldn't remember much about his childhood besides rigorous training and development of his skill. One time though, when he couldn't have been more than four, he vividly remembered crying after injuring himself. Drakkon attacked him, and held him against the wall with his pointed dragon's tail, telling him never to show human emotion again. And Tor never did. At least not in Drakkon's presence. But whether he liked to admit it or not, human emotion bubbled out of him sometimes, especially if he stayed in the mortal realm for too long. Almost like it couldn't be bottled up anymore.

And where he came from is another mystery. All the Guardians have been around for millennia. Yet, he grew up like a human would.

"You are my experiment. That's all you need to know," Drakkon told him the one-time Tor was brave enough to ask.

"Am I human?"

"Can a human travel the realms? Can a human control the mortal's atmosphere? Can a human be gifted with such deviant powers?" Then Drakkon chained him to the wailing wall of bones using hell's poisonous shackles. "If you can survive this, you'll learn not to ask such stupid questions again."

No, Drakkon had trained him well. Keeping a hardened expression no longer tormented Tor. No one else needed to know what thoughts went through his mind. So, Tor stopped asking questions. Until now.

The girls stepped into the younger one's tent, and the whispering started immediately.

"What happened? We saw you dead!"

"He tried to kill me, but I guess it didn't work. It was like my insides blew up. Then I woke up. Slowly, my body healed. I don't know what to make of it."

Her body healed itself? Obviously, she recovered, but Tor had toyed with the idea of someone helping her, aiding in her recovery.

But if her body had healed itself, Tor wondered what other kind of power her body contained.

Did Drakkon know this?

"How'd you get back here?"

Tor's attention was brought back to the whispered conversation.

"Th-this monster attacked me and tried to take my soul!" Marcy's voice shook even more.

"Him?" Mathilde pointed in Tor's direction.

All Marcy could do was shake her head. Finally, she explained, "It was the ugliest, most menacing demon I've ever seen."

"We don't ever see the demons," Mathilde said with a hint of fear in her voice.

"They're horrid." Marcy wrapped her arms around her body. "This one, in particular, wanted to steal my soul. I don't know what all would have happened, but I felt violated just by his menacing stare." She brought her hands to her face. "I can't even fathom what he wanted to do."

Tor felt a human emotion try to rear its head, but he shoved it back into place. He could not feel for this girl. Empathy was weakness.

"You're here now," the younger girl said. Tor could see them embrace.

It bubbled up from deep inside again, so he quickly looked away from the scene. Not now. He didn't want to deal with human emotion right now. This went beyond empathy. He could shove empathy back in place. But this…this was different. He knew exactly what this was. He'd felt it before. The times he entered the mortal realm. On the off chance, he observed a parent hugging their child.

Longing. One of the most powerful emotions he struggled with. He needed to do what he did in those circumstances, completely step away from the situation. Unfortunately, he couldn't step away from this Marcy. Just the same, he didn't have to watch the embrace.

"I think it's safe to say you're not just a Shadow."

"That's what I've been thinking, but what else could I be?"

"Well, think about it," the younger girl said. "If you were just a Shadow, you'd be dead. Twice…no, three times now."

Tor checked the area and noticed nothing unusual. This part of Levea was nothing like the other parts. Levea was the name for the area of hell where Drakkon kept the younger Shadows. He decided long ago to deceive them, so they unknowingly would sign pacts with Guardians when they were ready and more advanced in their skills to be of use. Guardians had the unfun job of keeping Shadows in line, so they were the only ones who ever crossed into Levea. Nothing in hell was peaceful, but this small portion of Levea where the Shadow trainees stayed at least didn't have the stench of hatred and the atmosphere of evil that seemed to be about every other level of Drakkon's realm.

The girls had been quiet for too long. He lifted the tent flap.

Marcy was whispering in the young girl's ear. The young girl nodded and whispered, "When?"

"Never," Tor said, seeing both girls jump. "Whatever you're thinking about doing, don't do it."

"You have no idea what we're discussing," Marcy snapped. "I happened to ask Mathilde when their next training expedition is, and she didn't quite hear me. So, relax." She did this eye roll thing that tempted Tor to freeze those blue eyes in place if he could access the elements here like he could in the mortal realm.

"You're lying," he said instead. "And planning something would be stupid."

"Thanks for your opinion."

Her dismissal was like a blow to the gut. Without thinking his fire flared as he let a large flame encircle his hand.

Mathilde was terrified; Marcy seemed more suspicious than anything else. Tor needed the upper hand, so he directed the flame at the younger girl, drawing out the human emotions in Marcy that he was just trying to squelch. It licked out at her. She screamed as Marcy shoved her down and stood in between the girl and the flame. Now Tor saw terror.

And it satisfied him. Somewhat.

He didn't want to hurt the girl, but this blue-eyed Shadow needed to learn a lesson. Because he may be a monster as she put it, but there were far worse. The sooner she learned to obey direct orders the better. "You defy me, and you won't be the only one to suffer. Do I make myself clear?"

Marcy nodded and whispered, "Okay. Please don't hurt her."

Tor lowered his arm, breathing deeply, immediately calming the flames. On the outside, that is. As Marcy stared at him with those eyes of hers, there was nothing he could do to quench the fire within.

13

Missing Person

There were only so many places to go in Levea, only so many Shadow trainees to visit, only so many insults to throw at the oh-I'm-so-cool-just-look-at-my-flames sourpuss standing outside of her tent. As Marcy lay on her cot, she realized that this was what Drakkon had meant to do all along.

Kill her with boredom.

She had a plan though. It had taken Tor's threatening Mathilde to bring Marcy to her senses. But no one could know her plan. She couldn't risk anyone getting hurt because of her.

But after deliberating, contemplating, deciding, and contriving her exact steps toward freedom for the last five nights, the only energy she could muster was breathing and the occasional blinking of her eyes.

Yep, Drakkon was trying to kill her with boredom.

Mathilde still came by every evening before leaving for the mortal realm, but she never stayed for long. Thanks to Mr. Fireballs out there.

Marcy itched to go with her, itched to get her hands on more mortal supplies, itched to get away. It would happen. She would bide her time. Let Tor think she had given in. It irked her that there was no way to outmaneuver or outrun him, so she figured she would just have to outsmart him. And in that, she was determined to be successful.

She heard someone approaching the tent from the back. Sitting up, she listened. Tor stepped around the tent. She heard his footsteps walk to the back. Something put her on edge. Something evil lurked behind the tent. Goosebumps shot out across her skin.

"What do you want?" Tor asked whoever or whatever approached the back of the tent.

"Drakkon wants to see you. I'm in charge now."

Marcy covered her mouth to contain her scream. Not Rakye. Not him.

But she knew it was. That's what she felt. More than his presence, she felt the tormented souls he had imprisoned.

What would he do to her?

She wasn't about to wait to find out. Throwing on some clothes, she bound her hair out of her face and slid into her boots. Levea contained no hiding places. At least not to the two outside her tent. Then she thought of Mathilde and how the young girl snuck out of Levea and into the other parts of hell.

Tor had a shadow, or at least his clothes did. She saw it herself. Now she wondered if there was any way to access his central circuitry. None of the demons could be accessed because they were so evil that they would immediately contaminate a Shadow, oftentimes killing them.

"I'm not sure that's a good idea," Tor said. "We know that self-control isn't in your bag of tricks."

"Don't worry about me, little boy. You might be Drakkon's pet, but you're one step away from me devouring you."

Tor laughed! Marcy had to give it to the guy. He had nerves of steel. "You try to lay a hand on me, Rakye. Go ahead and try. I would enjoy it." Marcy peaked out of the back tent opening and saw Tor lean into the monstrous demon. "I would rip you apart, limb by limb, and drop you into the bottomless torment pit."

"You're getting a little too big for your own good, Tor," Rakye said without the least bit of fear. "Watch your back. You might be Drakkon's pet now, but he won't protect you forever. And I, for one, look forward to that day. Now get out of my face and run to your master while I entertain the little lady."

Marcy didn't wait a second longer. She had to risk it.

Before talking herself out of it, she stepped into a shadow her lantern made and shifted to where Tor's shadow stormed away.

Tor passed through the barrier before Rakye noticed Marcy had disappeared. She breathed a sigh of relief. But only for a moment. The scene Tor had walked into stole Marcy's breath.

It was pitch black with horrendous screams that tore at Marcy's flesh. She began to shiver in fear. Tor stopped. Right in the middle of the dark atmosphere, he spoke, "What are you doing?"

Marcy wondered who he could be talking to. The screaming nearly drove her mad, but there was nothing she could do but stay in his shadow.

Then it hit her. In pitch darkness, could there be a shadow?

"This is not the place for you." Tor didn't move. "You realize that you're clinging to my shirt?"

Marcy looked down at where her hands would be. They clutched his shirt.

Tor still didn't move. "I'm not moving until you reveal yourself, Marcy."

She sighed. "If you already know I'm here, why do I need to reveal myself?"

He turned fast. Fast enough that Marcy lost her grip. Right when she noticed the blaze in his eyes, the darkness seemed to drag her in its arms and pull her in. Her scream joined the others. Tor reached out, grabbed her shirt, and yanked her to him. "This is not the place for you," he said again.

"I couldn't…" but she couldn't tell him how afraid she had been to stay with Rakye.

"I have to take you back." Tor grabbed her waist and began walking her back.

Even though the darkness and screams were too much, she still said, "No. Please. Let me stay with you. I won't be any trouble."

"You have no idea how much trouble you are."

"Please. Don't make me beg."

Tor stayed in place for a few seconds, only to keep walking toward the entrance and back to Rakye.

"Where is your heart? I know it's not of stone."

"You're right. My heart's not of stone. I don't have one."

Tor still held Marcy in front of him while he walked back. She clung to him but moved one hand and covered his heart. A heart thrumming with life.

He stopped and dropped her. The darkness wailed and sucked her into it.

"Tor!"

In what seemed like the last second before she was consumed, he yanked her again to him. "Don't ever do that again." His breathing was fast, his eyes burning into hers.

"I'm sorry," she whispered.

"There are no apologies here. Save it."

He stepped out of the darkness and back into Levea. Walking across the waterfall, he paused and sighed. Marcy turned her head and gasped. The entire camp had been destroyed. Her tent was shredded. Her personal items busted into a million pieces. Marcy heard Rakye roaring far off. "Where is she?"

"She's here," Tor called and pushed Marcy away from him.

"My stuff," she lamented. Everything had been destroyed. Marcy dropped to her knees and took in shaky breaths. From the dark place, she had experienced with Tor and now this, she could barely breathe.

"You should have stayed," Tor simply said.

Rakye appeared as the massive bird and roared at Marcy.

"Calm down," Tor said to Rakye. "I brought her back."

Rakye morphed into his hideous human form. "You stupid, pathetic girl."

"You ruined all of my stuff!" Marcy yelled, deciding tears

would get her nowhere. She'd have to save them for later.

Rakye tilted his head back and laughed. That evil laugh made Marcy's skin crawl.

"And I took her to the pit," Tor said to Rakye. "You should have seen her."

Rakye stopped long enough to say, "I would have loved to see that."

From Rakye to Tor, Marcy's fury boiled. The energy inside of her that she had felt heal her now flowed like a current. Her fingers tingled with the electricity. Before she knew what was happening, she held her hands out and shouted, "I've had enough!" The power left her body and hit Tor right in the chest, sending him flying into the air and down the waterfall. She turned on Rakye, but he saw what happened and threw himself on her to attack.

But the energy had a mind of its own. It threw him off her and into the air. He became a monstrous bird and flew at her; she held out her hands and threw him back. The bird screeched a wail that shook the trainee camp.

Someone from behind tackled Marcy to the ground, taking her by surprise. "Don't move," Tor ordered her.

It was then she noticed he was using fire, but she barely felt it.

This time, she was the one laughing.

14

Trust No One

As Rakye and Tor argued over what to do with Marcy, she observed trainees coming out from their hiding spots and looking at her with a mix of awe and trepidation. Marcy scanned the camp and grimaced. It had been completely leveled. Rakye definitely hadn't practiced any self-control. It dawned on her that there was a significant number of trainees missing. She turned to the two arguing and snapped, "Where are all the trainees?"

Both Rakye and Tor stopped, but neither answered.

Maybe it was because she was snarling at them. "I asked a question! Where is everyone? They should be back by now!"

Rakye leaned closer, and Marcy saw the souls screaming out. "You might know a few of them," he sneered.

Nausea rolled in Marcy, and she looked away. "I'm going to kill you."

Rakye grabbed her chin and forced her to look at him. "You're the one who's going to pay dearly."

"I don't care how long it takes. I will kill you." Marcy stared straight at him, the heat of her anger rolling in waves inside her.

"Take her with you to Drakkon," Rakye said to Tor. "He'll know what to do about her. That's if you can contain her. Your fire does nothing to her."

"Let's go," Tor said gruffly and pushed her away from Rakye.

"Until next time," Rakye said to her, flicking his tongue around in an obscene gesture.

"Step into my shadow. It's easier that way," Tor ordered.

"No," Marcy said and crossed her arms. "You can go to hell. Oh, wait, you're already there."

"I don't have time for this." Tor grabbed her with one arm and threw her toward the waterfall.

Marcy, once again, began to freefall down the length of the waterfall, screaming more in frustration than anything else. She had lost friends. She had lost her belongings. And now she had lost control because unfortunately, she didn't know how to move within levels the way Tor did. This meant she would fall until she hit something.

Only this time she didn't hit something, as much as she fell into something. Or someone.

"Put her in here."

Marcy tried to squirm her way out of the clutches of whatever monster had caught her. The creature held her from behind in a vice grip at arm's length. In new apparent terror, she kicked frantically but to no avail. Even though she was unable to see behind her, the creature's pungent smell of burnt flesh and decay reeked, and its paws that held her had blood dripping off of them.

When she paused long enough to glance ahead of her, she saw the cage. "No," she pleaded, losing all sense of pride. "No, please."

The cage was tall enough but thin. Marcy lost all composure, pleading and begging.

It didn't work.

The creature threw her in it and slammed the door in place. Now that she could see the creature, she backed away from it. She couldn't decide if it was a wolf or a man. It stood tall with the chest and arms of a man who had taken one too many steroid injections, but the hands and feet were blood-dripping paws, along with a wolf's head, long snout, and large, protruding fangs, also dripping blood. Now it leaned close to her and sniffed. "When can I have a bite?"

She backed away until she hit the back of the cage and then yowled in pain.

"You don't want to touch the bars, sweetheart." The voice cooed at her, and a cold fear filled her. She turned in the direction of Drakkon. "They're made from the embers of hell, and even if they won't disintegrate you, it won't exactly feel pleasant."

"What do you want from me?" She wiped at her eyes and used her sleeve to wipe at her running nose.

"Ah, the pleasantries are over." He signaled the wolf-man who pushed the cage toward the ledge. The ledge that fell into the burning inferno of hell.

"Stop!" she shouted. "I'll do whatever you want!"

With one final push, the cage fell off the ledge. She screamed until her throat was raw, only to notice the cage didn't fall into the flames. The flames licked at the bottom of the cage, but somehow it hung in the air, hovering above the torment.

Already the heat had become too much. She turned around in quick movements, trying to figure out any way of escape.

Then she saw the other cage.

With Mathilde in it.

"Marcy!" the girl cried out to her.

"Mathilde!"

Panic rose inside of Marcy. How could she save her friend?

She turned to look back at the ledge where a host of demons stood, watching. Drakkon acted entertained, looking from cage to the next with a schoolyard grin on his beautiful face. Tor stood next to him, and Marcy's eyes locked into his. Was there fear in his eyes? Empathy? No, nothing. He watched her with the same coldness as the other monsters.

"Here's what's going to happen," Drakkon said giddily. "One of you will fall to your eternal torment. One of you will not."

Marcy swallowed hard and glanced at Mathilde. She wasn't about to let her mentee die. One touch of the flames of hell, and Mathilde would disintegrate. Maybe with Marcy's newfound internal energy, she could find a way out.

"Unless Marcy, you're ready to make a deal."

Marcy didn't respond. She knew the deal wouldn't be good.

"Serve me."

Drakkon's mouth hadn't seemed to move, but the words echoed in the depths of hell.

Glancing around her, she felt the evil permeate in the air, a palpable sensation that sent whatever energy was harnessed inside of her to flow in response. The answer came out, yet she didn't know she had said it until it echoed behind Drakkon's words.

"No."

There was a collective gasp. Marcy acted just as surprised. She hurriedly added, "Not until you release Mathilde and promise not to harm her."

"Then you will serve me?"

The energy inside of her revolted again, but this time she pressed her lips together until she could control her words. "Release her. Now."

Drakkon watched Marcy for a long time. Marcy matched his gaze. Finally, he nodded. Mathilde's cage moved toward the ledge. The wolf-man pulled the black rope to him, which was connected to the top of the cage.

An idea formed in Marcy's mind.

"Tor, take her back to the other shadow slaves," Drakkon was saying.

Tor glanced briefly at Marcy before grabbing Mathilde. "There are no shadows down here, so you'll have to hold on." He created a blue mist and walked through it.

"A promise is a promise. Are you ready to sign?"

"One more thing…"

"No! Sign your name in blood or be damned!" His image kept flickering between the male form and the dragon.

"Either I die or I'm a slave for eternity, so I think you can answer a couple of questions!"

"Or I can drop you into hell! And trust me, you never die. You will be tormented forever. That's how hell works."

"But you need me, so that won't happen."

He stopped and glared at her. None of the demons moved. Marcy could sense their shock that she would dare to even negotiate with Drakkon. But, she didn't have a lot of options. Hanging over the flames of hell created a whole new perspective for Marcy.

Drakkon could have done this all along. He could have captured her and thrown her into this torment pit. There's absolutely no escape. Yet he hadn't.

Why?

Marcy was beginning to realize the simple answer.

Drakkon needed her.

Whatever was going on inside of her. The energy. The healing power. The shield. Drakkon must have realized how strong Marcy was. What she might be capable of with the proper training.

The problem for Drakkon was that he wasn't the only one with that realization. Marcy had figured it out, too.

"I want to know why I am so different from everyone else."

Drakkon acted surprised. "That's it? That's what you want to know?"

"Yes. Am I a Shadow? A human? A demon? What am I?"

"A Shadow," he said with a shrug. "That's the mystery. You're a Shadow with extraordinary abilities. It happens occasionally.

Those like you make the best warriors."

Marcy felt disappointed but not for long. Drakkon was lying. Felt the lie as it reached her ears. Either Drakkon didn't know the answer, or he did, and he wasn't going to say.

"So? I fulfilled my side of the bargain," Drakkon said. "Will you serve me? Do I have your complete loyalty?"

Marcy's mouth couldn't bring out any words. She was already faint from being so close to the heat. Sheer will kept her standing.

Suddenly, Lynde appeared along with a host of guardians. "Sir, we need full legions immediately."

Drakkon did not move his gaze from Marcy's.

"Sir? The nuclear bomb is set to detonate. There will be thousands of mortal souls, maybe even millions, flooding our gates."

Drakkon let out a breath. "Fine. Stay here and watch her." Before Lynde could contest, Drakkon said to Marcy, "I will be back soon. You better have the right answer."

Marcy felt her first glimmer of hope. She handled Lynde before; he would be a piece of cake. The wolf-man stayed behind, too. That might be a problem. But if she could use that force inside her as she did with Tor and Rakye, she could immobilize them long enough to make a break for it. But where would she go? Was there even a way out?

The minute Drakkon left with the group of demons trailing after him, Lynde drew his sword and sliced the wolf-man in two, shoving him off the ledge and into the inferno. Then the Guardian looked over at Marcy.

Marcy's mouth dropped open. He was going to kill her this time by sword. The sword containing hell's poison. The blaze of hell licked at the bottom of the cage, and she contemplated what to do next. "I know that you and I have our issues."

He grabbed the lever and yanked on the black chord, and the cage jolted toward the ledge. Even with the wolf-man's muscles, Lynde's strength had to be far greater because he had the cage on the ground past the ledge in two swift pulls.

"Drakkon will be furious. He needs me on his side." Marcy couldn't believe she was using Drakkon as an excuse to save her life. When that didn't work, Marcy, still in shock from Lynde's actions with wolf-man, tried to summon up the energy from within. She needed to hurry or Lynde would slice her, too. But she was nervous. She closed her eyes tight and tried to focus. If only she could stop shaking.

Lynde already had the door of the cage thrown open.

Marcy raised her hands at the looming Guardian. "Don't," she warned.

He reached in and snatched her. "We don't have time. Now listen closely. You need to agree to sign your allegiance with Drakkon. Do you understand?"

Marcy floundered over words. "Wh-Wh-What? You're not going to kill me?" It was then she noticed his eyes were no longer flames but deep blue. They held each other's gaze for the briefest moment. This Guardian opened his mouth to say something, then he closed it. "What? Tell me."

"I need you to do as I say. Sign your allegiance." In a lowered voice, he whispered, "It won't be binding. Make sure to grab the writing instrument from my hand, and my hand only. Do you understand?"

He opened up the blue mist and grabbing Marcy's hand, stepped through it.

They walked toward where her tent used to be. Tor stood near the remains and looked shocked when he saw Marcy with Lynde.

"Here," Lynde said and threw Marcy toward Tor. "She gave her allegiance. Drakkon ordered you to watch her for the time being."

Tor nodded slowly. "She agreed?" He didn't mask his surprise.

"Isn't that what I said? Now here, take her and watch her. Drakkon's orders. I need to get back to the ranks," Lynde said.

"I'll take it from here," Tor told him.

Lynde gave Marcy a brief look before walking away. The energy inside of her started bubbling in excitement as if it recognized what he was trying to communicate. He wanted Marcy to do what he said.

Why? Was Lynde trying to revolt against Drakkon? Did he want Marcy to side with him?

All Marcy knew was that anything was better than that cage. If she had to pretend to join the ranks, then so be it. What was going to be even more difficult than that was to be around Tor. He had betrayed her one too many times. First, he tried to kill her. Then, he tricked her into thinking she was going with him undetected, only to take her to the dark pit of despair, then he threw her into hell and into the hands of the wolf-man and Drakkon.

They eyed each other warily. Marcy decided right then and there. She didn't know what Lynde was up to, but he did just rescue her from the cage. She would follow his plan until her plan could come to light. And no matter what, she vowed to herself that she would never, *ever*, trust Tor.

15

Cleaning Up the Mess

Tor assisted Marcy in fixing up the trainee's camp. He told himself it was out of sheer boredom.

But that was a lie, and he knew it.

Something had happened when he watched Marcy dangle inside that cage. He couldn't escape the grief that had encompassed him. He had to fight the desire to rescue her. Nor could he deny the complete relief he felt when he saw her with Lynde. He thought she would never pledge allegiance to Drakkon, but at least she made it out alive.

What in the world was going on with him? One minute he's killing her, and the next minute he's relieved she's alive. He had mastered human emotion. Until her.

He didn't get attached to anyone. Ever. Especially not some emotional hothead girl who could throw him off the camp's ledge and down the waterfall, who would laugh at a full-fledged demon like Rakye, who had enough guts to look directly at Drakkon and tell him no, who had enough nerve to put her hand over Tor's beating heart. The heart he tried to deny was there.

"Tor?"

He glanced up at Marcy standing over him.

"There's nothing here," she said.

He was crouched down, going through items that might still be useful. He looked at what he was holding in his hand, then threw it down. He nodded stiffly. This apparent loss for words had come over him since Lynde brought her back.

"I'm going to go check on Mathilde."

That was another thing. Why was she acting so polite? Would she become a Shadow slave? Or, would she would be his equal? That brought up the nagging thought about Drakkon using her to take Tor's place.

Tor pushed the thought aside. This had been the right outcome. Drakkon wanted Tor to train her. The least he could be was somewhat civil, not that civility was a thing in hell. Still, he nodded again. "Hurry. If the mortal realm's world war is upon us, we should get you trained in some basic soldier techniques as soon as possible."

Marcy went to say something, but stopped, shoved her hands in her pockets, and walked away.

With her back to him, he watched her and let the curiosity turn to a longing. No need to be guarded when she wasn't watching. He sat still crouched among the ruins of the trainee's camp and wondered how in the world he was supposed to keep this longing in check. He needed to stop it before it grew into something dangerous. Drakkon would use this emotion against Tor.

Mathilde came out of a half-standing bunker tent, and the two girls embraced.

"She's pretty, isn't she?"

Tor stood up and formed a fireball in a split second, aiming it at the voice.

"I'm s-s-sorry," the teen trainee said with hands up in surrender, stepping back.

Tor felt the flames rise in him. How dare this stupid trainee walk up to him like a comrade? Like an equal? But if he showed his anger, would it prove his guilt? He finally decided the best course of action was to let the teen trainee go. He lowered his arm and extinguished the fire. "Don't ever do that again," he warned.

"I'm s-s-sorry," the teen stumbled over his apology for the second time. "I thought you heard me approach you."

"I did," Tor lied. "I just couldn't believe you'd have the nerve to do so." He made sure to layer on the scorn and condemnation. "Who are you, and why did you approach?"

"Arec," the trainee said. "I'm friends with Marcy. I heard she joined the ranks, and I wanted to see if it was true. I just got back from the mortal realm, so I thought I'd check on her."

"She joined the ranks."

"Is it true she threw you—?" Arec stopped himself. Tor made sure the fire ignited in his palms to indicate not to bring it up.

"We took care of Marcy and made sure she signed."

For a brief moment, a look of anger washed over the boy's face, but it was fleeting. "When does she leave?"

"Arec!" Marcy called his name. She ran to him, and they embraced.

Tor had to focus to contain his flames, which peaked without his intention. That would be a problem. Too much was happening to him. He turned and focused on something other than the two's conversation.

"I heard you had quite the day," Arec whispered.

"You have no idea."

"We were both in cages over an inferno," Mathilde answered. "It was horrendous. There are some freaky aspects that we never imagined."

"So, is it true? You joined the ranks?" Arec didn't hide his disappointment.

Tor found his attention back on the group. His attention was mostly on Marcy. She was like a magnet, and he could no longer look away.

"She had to," Mathilde said for Marcy. "She had to save me from the fire." The young girl looked at Marcy with such reverence and appreciation that Marcy blushed.

"Look at this place," another Shadow trainee approached the group. "I just got back from the only tents still standing."

"Is yours one of them?" Marcy asked the girl.

"Yes, why?"

"Do you have any water left? I need to clean up."

"Sure. Do you have any of your mortal shampoos or soaps?"

"No, Rakye destroyed everything of mine."

"How many souls of ours did he steal?" Arec asked.

"Too many." Marcy visibly shuddered. "Why don't you gather

everyone who's here and start rebuilding as much as we can salvage," she said to Arec. "As soon as I'm clean, I'll come back to help."

"Don't think so," Tor said and walked up to the group. "We need to start training immediately. This place is going to take a lot of work to fix up, and we don't have the time. And really, it doesn't matter. No one cares that your human paraphernalia didn't make it."

The three of them didn't speak. Eventually, Marcy said, "It mattered to us. Now if you'll excuse me, I'm going to wash up."

Tor furrowed his eyebrows to keep an angry expression on his face, but he felt embarrassed at saying something so hurtful. "Hurry." He turned from them and tried to get a handle on the emotions. He never used to care about Shadows, and especially not the trainees, but now it bothered him that he said something hurtful.

"Marcy?" Arec called out to her.

She turned around. "Yeah?"

"Don't forget to say goodbye."

"I won't." To the girl, she said, "He'll make a good leader. Take care of him, Tiya."

"He's been worried about you," Tiya said shyly. "It's evident where his affections lie."

"No, don't say that," Marcy said. "We've all been friends since, well, since as long as I can remember. He's like a brother."

"Technically, he is our brother."

The girls giggled.

"Honestly, we've been protected here in this part of Levea. I'm not sure that love exists in this place," Marcy said.

"Is it bad in other parts of Levea? How bad?"

"Not just bad. Evil. I can see why it takes a toll on Elder Shadows."

"Don't let it do that to you. I don't want you to change."

"It won't," Marcy said quickly. "I will do everything in my power not to let the evil in this place contaminate me."

Tor had stayed quiet during their conversation, but he silently agreed with Marcy. He couldn't see her transforming like the other Shadows. There was a rare beauty to her that Tor hoped hell did not extinguish. He told himself not to think this way. The only beauty in hell was false, a deception to trick subordinates into submission.

"Hello?" Marcy said.

Tor realized she was speaking to him. "What?"

"I'm going inside to wash up. You're going to stay out here, right?"

Oh, the desire. It was like honey in his veins. But his countenance revealed nothing. "I've already seen you naked, but if you want to keep up pretenses, go right ahead."

Marcy went inside the other trainee's tent without a response. Tor had hoped for one. Still, the tent flap remained open. Tor found himself gazing in.

The other trainee—Tiya—gave her some clothes and a jug of water. "Remember when I stole this shirt with you? You trained me well." Tiya stepped outside and noticed Tor. "It was just the one time."

"Right," he said. "How else would you get mortal paraphernalia?"

Marcy zipped the tent closed. After several minutes, Tor nearly went in to see what was taking so long. But he didn't have to because the tent opened and she came out. "I'm ready."

She looked fresh and clean.

"Let's go," he said gruffly.

"Don't you…want to…" Marcy pointed in the tent. "Wash up?"

Tor could feel the heat rise off his skin. Was this what embarrassment felt like? He tried to keep clean. The filth of this place disgusted him. Could he be that bad?

"We've had a busy day, and the inferno was hot. I saved you some water. Do you want to wash up or not?"

"I'll take care of myself later. I can't have you running off. And I don't think cleanliness is very high on anyone's priority list once they join the ranks."

"Well, I will always be clean."

"Good."

"Why do you care? You hang out with a lot worse than me."

"I mean that if I'm the one that's going to be training you, it will be nice for you not to stink."

"Ditto."

He looked down at himself. "Okay, I admit my shirt is nasty. It needs to be thrown in the inferno." He glanced at her and saw her troubled expression. "What's wrong?"

"Nothing."

He felt the lie as it left her lips. A slight shift in her mood. Her guard was up again. He wanted desperately to continue the conversation. But she pressed her lips together and completely turned from him. He walked to her. "Marcy."

"What?" She kept her back to him.

"I've been in that cage before, too." Tor tried not to think about it. But when he had to watch Marcy and Mathilde in those cages, all the nightmarish memories came flooding back.

"You have?" She slowly turned to face him.

"Yes. Drakkon enjoys that torture device. Except I was a child. Not even a young man. Younger than Mathilde. And my only crime was questioning where I came from."

"So that's when you became all angry and nasty," Marcy said quietly, more to herself, before walking outside the tent. "Well, let's go. I guess I need to train."

Tor could see the wall she built inside of herself. He told himself it was a good thing. She shouldn't trust anyone here. Especially him. He had had orders to kill her. He had to put her in her place to break her defiance. There was no way he could ever express anything more for her than civility during training. And it would break him if she started to trust him, only to get orders to kill her again.

So even though he wanted to shatter that wall she built to protect herself, she was already learning how to adapt in hell.

16

Decisions

Tor wielded the sword in basic moves. He stopped to make sure she was paying attention.

Marcy looked at him in a you've-got-to-be-kidding-me expression. "I have to hold a sword? Like as I'm a Guardian now?"

"I don't know in what capacity you'll be used." Tor shrugged. "But probably a Guardian. Or Shadow Master."

"Shadow Master? Like an Elder Shadow?"

"No. There are no more Shadow Masters because the Shadows seem to die before Drakkon can ever elevate them to that position."

"Most shadows die?" She seemed fixated on that point.

"Pretty much."

"How? I mean, I know a Guardian can disintegrate them, but I always thought that maybe we were somewhat useful."

"Their Guardian kills them for a lot of reasons, or they kill themselves. They're a depressive lot."

"Why do their Guardians kill them? And why do they kill themselves?" She seemed to be getting worked up. "We're ordered around, and then we do the job, and we still get killed? That doesn't sound fair."

"We're in hell. Nothing's fair." Tor couldn't hide the sarcasm.

He changed his tone and added, "Guardians kill them because they don't do their job correctly. Sometimes a Shadow will try to alter human destiny that goes against orders. And they kill themselves because like I just said, they're a depressive bunch of half-breeds."

Marcy gasped.

Wrong move, Tor.

"Half-breeds? What are *you*? You look like a human, too!"

"Maybe I'm a half-breed, too. Unfortunately, I have no idea who I am or where I came from. Other than Drakkon said I'm a Storm-Maker and currently a Guardian at the moment. So, here I am. At your service. Now pay attention."

"So, chances are I'm going to become depressed and die?"

"Not as a Shadow Master. You have special talents that no other Shadow has. Listen, I don't know, okay? I'm just trying to do my job and train you."

"That must bother you, huh? What were you doing before babysitting me?"

Tor sighed, trying to keep his exasperation in check. This could be a good thing though. The more annoying she acted, the less he fantasized about her. "I already told you. I was a Storm-Maker. I'm not exactly a Guardian. I'm just a heck-of-a lot-stronger than they are, so Drakkon told me to…"

"…kill me?"

Tor shrugged. "An order is an order."

Marcy groaned in frustration. "An order is an order? Really. What about saying, 'Drakkon, what did this Shadow trainee ever do? Let's give her a chance.' What is wrong with people here?"

"First of all, get this through your stubborn head: there are no *people* in hell. At least not mortals. This place is to house the mortals who die. They serve Drakkon while they're alive, and he welcomes them here when they're dead. All of the rest of us are spirit beings. Seriously? Did no one ever teach you this?"

Marcy put her hands up. "You know what? It doesn't matter. It sucks." She stopped and breathed in and out. Tor saw that she was trying to keep her emotions in check. That used to bother him, but now…now, it gave him a huge lump in his throat. "It sucks," she said again. "That we don't have a say. I want to be free like the mortals. I want to choose my path. Not be forced into servitude because if not, I'll be thrown into the inferno."

Tor walked over to her and said quietly, "You have to stop thinking like that, Marcy. It'll do you no good. For whatever reason, we're here."

"This doesn't look like training to me," Drakkon said from behind Tor.

"I was just telling Marcy to remember her place, sir." Tor turned and faced Drakkon, lowering his head in standard submissive form.

"Yes. Has our student not figured it out yet?"

"She has come a long way from before."

"The inferno does a good job of reinforcing our mission, doesn't it, Tor?"

"Yes, sir."

"Marcy, darling," Drakkon eyed her carefully. "Lynde told me that you've sworn your allegiance and are ready to bind your service to me?"

Tor looked at Marcy from the corner of his eyes. She seemed to have difficulty saying, "Yes, sir." If Tor had thought about it, he would have warned her to watch her facial expressions. He couldn't imagine seeing her in the cage again.

"Well, then, we have a ceremony to attend." Drakkon flicked his wrist and an opening to his throne presented itself.

Tor indicated for Marcy to walk through. He pointed his sword at her to warn her to move. She looked at him with fear and hostility, then marched through the opening. Tor moved to follow her, but Drakkon reached out and stopped him.

"You have not forgotten your assignment, have you?"

"No, sir." Tor didn't want to think about what Drakkon's ultimate goal was for Marcy.

"Everything is working out perfectly. I would hate to be disappointed in you." Drakkon's words were low and full of implications.

"I will not disappoint you."

"Of course, you won't," Drakkon said. "You know better than that. She needs to choose you as her Guardian. Has she softened on you yet?"

"A little. It is hard being civil to an emotional girl, but she's responded well so far."

"Good. Once I have you both together, the real torture, I mean the real training, can begin. By the way, where's your shirt?"

"It was filthy."

Drakkon raised his eyebrows. "Be careful. You are to change her. Not the other way around. I wouldn't enjoy the destruction of two of the most talented subjects I've had. Then again, maybe I would." He walked through the opening, and Tor followed.

Marcy's words repeated in his mind. *It sucks that we don't have a say.*

Tor mentally shook himself. He could not think like that. He could not afford to. He only had to remember Drakkon's torture to know that Marcy's way of thinking was dangerous. And the quicker he got Marcy to see that, the better.

The throne room was full of all the dimwits. He hated the demons. They were good at torture and unspeakable evils, but that was their only skill. They hated him, too. He was far more intelligent and dangerous. And Marcy was right. They all stank.

Tor observed Marcy standing in the middle of the throne room, facing Drakkon now sitting on his throne. The pledge book lay in front of her, thick from the signatures of mortals and spirit beings through thousands of millennia.

He knew this was for the best, but he thought of her fierce independence and inwardly cringed at her pledging her existence to Drakkon's orders. This shouldn't be for her. She stood out like a flower among a dung pile. Beautiful and graceful. Her expression stone, her head held high. Servitude had to be better than eternal torture, right? All of a sudden, Tor wasn't so sure.

"Guardians, approach."

The handful of Guardians that were selected to come to the ceremony stepped forward. Tor followed suit. He made his way to where Marcy stood. She watched him and the others warily.

"Your service is to me," Drakkon said to Marcy. "The Guardians will be over you as your protectors and trainers. Any order from them is an order from me unless I say otherwise. Do you understand?"

"Yes, sir." Marcy didn't bow her head. She stared at Drakkon with poorly masked resentment.

"Pick your Guardian carefully. Whatever one you choose will draw your blood for the blood oath. Sign your name in the book. Whatever Guardian you choose will be your secondary master, second only to me, of course."

Tor extended his left hand, which was the custom, as did the others. He wondered if she would choose him. The thought worried and thrilled him. If she chose someone else, she would no doubt be subjected to cruelty in her training. Tor knew he hadn't been nice, but he would at least try to be civil to her, especially since Drakkon wanted them together. But would she choose him? And what would be Tor's punishment if she didn't?

Tor was so lost in his thoughts, that the gasp from the crowd surprised him. When he saw what happened, his eyes nearly fell out of his head.

Marcy had chosen Lynde.

17

Wrong Moves

Marcy felt like she would throw up.

The Guardians stood in front of her, more like towered in front of her, in such an intimidating way that it was all she could do not to cower.

She glanced at the book, and the energy inside of her immediately revolted. That was almost as bothersome as any of this other stuff. The energy seemed to have a mind of its own. It flowed more freely now than ever. A part of her wanted to try it out, but if it faltered like it did in the cage, well, the outcome wouldn't be good.

It seemed to communicate with her, too. As her eyes scanned over the Guardians, it revolted against each one as a quick shock to her heart. Until Lynde.

She hadn't been too sure about actually following his directions until she felt the thrum of the energy when her gaze met his. Her arm outstretched before she knew what she was doing. The collective gasp surprised her. Tor didn't hide his surprise very well.

Ha! Okay, that felt good, too. The jerk. Like she would choose him. While he watched her dangle over the inferno, or after he nearly destroyed her with his fire.

It was confusing how civil he was being to her, but she refused to be swayed. She knew he was nothing but a coward. A true follower of Drakkon. And no matter what, even without Lynde's directions, her heart would never bow to the evil lord.

When Lynde's hand took hers, a current released within the two of them. Marcy stared at their hands and glanced back up at Lynde. He did a barely observed shake of his head. Marcy understood. Play along.

Whatever was happening, the energy inside of her meant her well. It had healed her and protected her from attacks, so even though she was unsure of Lynde's motives, if the energy was directing her to him, he was the safest bet as any.

"Lynde?" Drakkon tried not to sound surprised or disappointed, but Marcy heard both.

"I choose Lynde," she said, making sure not to look at Tor.

Drakkon recovered with a smile. "Lynde, you have been chosen to be master over Marcy. Do you accept?"

"I accept," he said with a sneer. He watched her with a dangerous glint in his eye.

"Seal the match with a blood promise."

Marcy became even more nervous. He told her to choose his writing device, but there was only one long, black feather laying against the book. Lynde reached for it. Marcy saw the tip was a razor-sharp point. He sliced her hand, and the demons started to get excited. Even Drakkon watched hungrily.

She wanted to step back. She didn't want to sign the book. She didn't want to become like these monsters. Lynde handed her the black feather, dripping with her blood.

A lump formed in her throat. She had been duped. Lynde tricked her. She would sign the book with her blood. She would be bound to Drakkon for eternity.

"Sign the book," Lynde ordered.

Just thinking about the inferno again had her reaching for the black feather. She noticed her hand had already healed. She hoped no one had noticed. As she thought about it, she realized that she had felt no pain. Wouldn't slicing her hand inflict a searing agony? At least for a moment?

The energy within her didn't seem threatened. Not that she was an expert at reading it just yet. Still, she didn't see any choice in the matter.

She signed her mark.

The demons were in a frenzy.

Drakkon stood at the throne with Lynde directly under him. The other Guardians had stepped aside. "Bow before your masters."

Now the energy revolted. It became rigid inside of her. She didn't want to bow either, but once again, she didn't see any other option. She pushed past the energy and fell to her knees.

"It is finally done," Drakkon shouted to the demonic crowd. "The final piece has been put into place. The destruction of mankind is finally upon us. I will get my revenge. I will destroy what He holds dear. I will inflict my vengeance onto those loyal to Him. I will take my rightful place. I will become the Most High."

Marcy shot up from her kneeling position. Well, the energy shocked her into standing. Luckily there was such chaos, and Drakkon was too busy basking in his power, that no one saw her reaction. Other than Lynde. Who watched her in stone silence. Neither of them shouted or cheered. And she thought of how, even with his scars and disfigurements, he stood out as such a stark contrast to all the others.

Almost as if he didn't belong there. The energy inside of her hummed in agreement.

"Surprise, surprise, surprise," Lynde said to Tor. "She didn't select you."

The throne room had been cleared with Drakkon ordering Lynde, Tor, and Marcy to stay behind.

"He's tried to kill me numerous times," Marcy said. "You've only tried to kill me once. The choice was clear."

"Good luck with her," Tor sneered at Lynde. "She's a pain. I'm glad to be done with her."

Marcy's anger riled up. "No one's more thrilled than I am."

"Interesting." Drakkon approached them. "I must admit I wondered that, as well, at the time of the selection, yet Marcy, you do make a good point. Tor's mission was to kill you. But now that you have pledged your loyalty, the hostility can be taken to the training field. Lynde?"

"Sir?"

"Tor will accompany you. It probably has not escaped your notice that these two are very rare spirit beings."

"I can handle her."

"You will have all eternity to mold her into your creation. Tor will need to be there at first to train her in a distinct form of combat that not even you are privy to."

The fire surged in Lynde.

"Calm down," Drakkon said. "Trust me, you will be glad she is at your side. Until then, Tor travels with you to train. Tor?"

"Sir?"

"Your time is limited. We need another atmospheric catastrophe. Be quick with this." Drakkon gave Tor a look that definitely had another meaning. "And Marcy?"

"Yeah…?"

Drakkon stared hard at her.

"Sir?"

Now he smiled. "I only wanted to welcome you among my legions. I'm glad I could persuade you to join. We will work well together."

"In what capacity, sir?"

"We will get to that. Until then, learn the art of torture, the skill of fighting, and the act of manipulation. You will need all of them. To the training fields," Drakkon ordered.

Lynde and Tor both extended a mist. Lynde glowered at Tor and said, "She's mine, remember?" Tor quickly extinguished his mist.

"Walk through," Lynde ordered Marcy.

Marcy held her head high and walked through the mist and into a lush field with rolling hills and a gentle breeze. She nearly cried in relief. The mortal realm. She felt the heartbeat of the Earth beat inside of her soul and welcomed it. She breathed in deep gulps of crisp air, tipped her head back, and took in the blue sky with patches of white clouds. Wrapping her arms around herself, she couldn't hide the smile. The first in a long time. "I never thought I'd come back," she whispered to herself, shivering at the horrors she had encountered in hell.

"We have to talk," Lynde said to her. "Alone."

"This is not the training field," Tor said from behind them. "Where are we?"

Marcy met Lynde's gaze and nodded. This was it. Somehow, Lynde had information. She felt it.

"Don't ignore me," Tor demanded, coming between them. "This is not the training field. Explain yourself."

Even with Tor's height, Lynde easily looked down on him. "I don't have to explain anything to you. This is where I chose to go. Now do what you need to do and get out of here."

"You act like she can be trained in a day," Tor said and shook his head. "Fine, let's get on with it."

"She doesn't need training with you," Lynde said, turning back to Marcy. "If anything, she could rip you apart in seconds."

Marcy's eyes widened in surprise. "Say what?"

Tor laughed.

Lynde's steely gaze bore into her. "You heard me. You could

take this jerk without barely breaking a sweat. Or at least you used to be able to."

Marcy swallowed, not knowing what to think. Tor didn't act confused at all. Only irritated. Then again, that seemed to be a permanent fixture on his face.

"Since you're so confident of your Shadow's abilities, then I suggest we move on to simulated attacks." Tor glanced at Marcy with an arrogant smirk playing on his lips.

"She's all yours." Lynde sat on the ground, picked a blade of grass, and placed it in his mouth. Marcy couldn't decide what to think. Here sat this Behemoth monster on the grass with legs crossed, relaxing.

"What are you doing?" Marcy asked.

"What does it look like I'm doing? I'm taking a load off, getting ready to watch what's going to be a fascinating spectacle."

Marcy crouched in front of him, her back to Tor. "I don't know how to fight him," she whispered.

Lynde rolled the blade of grass that stuck out of his mouth back and forth. Scars lined his features, his nose unnaturally bent, his eyebrows stuck out thick and unruly, yet his eyes were now the same blue as hers. "You need to remember," he stated. "The best way for that to happen is for you to fight. It seems that's when your natural elements come out."

"Remember what?" Tor asked from behind Marcy. She hadn't realized he'd walked behind her.

"None of your business, boy." Lynde didn't hide his loathing of

Tor.

That at least gave her one thing in common with her new Guardian. She stood up and wiped her hands on her pants. "So, what fight do we do?" She sounded braver than she felt. Marcy knew what Tor was capable of, and it bothered her what else he might be capable of doing that she hadn't even observed.

"Fire," Lynde said. "Let's start with that."

Tor still stared at Lynde with apparent fury. "You want fire?"

Oh no, Marcy thought. *That does not sound good.* "Wait, give me a few seconds to—"

But Tor already had a fireball in his hand. He hurled it at Marcy. The sheer force of it picked her up and threw her back, igniting her in the process. She landed engulfed in flames. She would have screamed, but the fall had taken her breath away.

Strangely enough, once she got her wind back, she sat up in shock. The flames were on her, yet they weren't devouring her. She felt the heat, but nothing more. So, she stood up. Eventually, the fire fizzed out, leaving steam rising from her clothes.

She heard Lynde still on the grass, laughing in delight. She cracked a grin until her eyesight landed on Tor. He marched toward her consumed in flames, fireballs in both hands. And then he let loose.

"Dodge them!" Lynde shouted.

But Marcy heard it too late. One after another, fireballs hit her. At least this time she held her feet in place, taking the brunt of the attack while standing up. Until Tor threw himself on her.

They tumbled in the grass, Tor holding her down, trying to breathe fire into her mouth. This time, she was fast enough. She shut her mouth and willed the energy to force him off her. She felt it rise in her, rolling, gaining momentum as if it had been waiting for her release. Without thinking, she rammed him in the groin. He released her hands, and she slammed them against his chest throwing him across the field.

She pushed herself up on all fours, suddenly very sore and tired. The flames might not get to her, but that was the second time the wind had been knocked out of her. Marcy needed to catch her breath.

No can do. Tor sailed in the air; sword unsheathed.

The energy inside thrummed, and Marcy rolled out of the way with only a second to spare. "I don't have any weapon!" she yelled in fury. She picked up rocks to throw at him, but he blocked them with a flick of the wrist. He charged again, sword coming right toward her.

She screamed and ran. Suddenly Tor stood in front of her and with a wicked grin said, "Gotcha," right before slicing her with the sword.

The pain was intense and immediate. He seemed to realize what he'd done because he dropped the sword and the flames that had surrounded him had disappeared.

But Marcy had already fallen on her knees, holding her stomach where the sword had sliced her. She glanced down and saw the blood right before she crashed onto her face and blacked out.

Marcy struggled into consciousness and groaned. The pain hadn't abated.

"Come on," Lynde said. "It's just a scratch. Sit up."

It sounded like he was in a tunnel far away. Marcy turned her head and blinked open her eyes. A fire blazed in front of her, and she immediately panicked. She tried to slide back away from it only igniting the dizzying pain again. She cried out.

"This fire isn't going to attack you," Lynde said. "It's to help keep you warm. Nights here can be cold."

"I don't like training, especially with an evil monster." Marcy wondered if she wasn't supposed to talk candidly with a Guardian, but the words fell out of her mouth before she could stop them.

Lynde didn't say anything at first. "I know, and I'm sorry. I'm grasping at anything that'll shake off the remnants of hell."

Did he just apologize? Marcy thought there were no apologies in hell? "Are you from hell?"

Lynde glanced at her, then looked away. "There is a lot I can't say right now because we're still playing their game. I only ask that you trust me." He leaned over and whispered in Marcy's ear. "You are safe with me."

"I was just stabbed with a sword," she whispered back.

It was then she noticed their faces were inches from each other. Not that either of them moved. Was this what desire felt like? Why was she wondering what it would be like to kiss him? Gently,

Lynde placed his hand over the injury. The warmth radiated through her. "One day soon, you'll know who I really am, and that I'm not an evil monster."

"I'd like that," she breathed, her insides on fire. Not in a bad way. No, not at all. "I wasn't referring to you as the evil monster. You didn't stab me."

Guilt clouded his expression, and he pulled away. Marcy immediately fell the chill from the absence of his touch. "I thought that his attacks would help…" Lynde paused as if choosing his next words. "This is so frustrating because there is so much to explain, but there are listening ears. I have to keep playing the part. You do too."

"Does that mean I have to keep getting killed?" Even though it hurt to move, she turned to the other side only to stop and stare straight up. The sky formed a big dome around her, the stars shone with brilliance as if someone scattered twinkle lights across the sky. She took a sharp breath of amazement. "It's gorgeous," she whispered. Levea—the part of hell where the trainees stayed— never had this amazing sky. More like a dense fog that hung above the atmosphere. "How far up does it go?" She stopped talking. Was she supposed to speak this freely to Lynde? He confused her. One minute he's gruff with an evil glint in his eyes, and the next minute he's built a fire to keep her warm and starting a fire inside of her that had yet to quenched.

"You never noticed the night sky on your many trips into the mortal realm?" he asked.

"Yes, but not for long. We had a strict schedule, and I had to save time to, you know, restock my supplies."

"Steal."

"Yeah. Which reminds me, will I have time to *restock*? Rakye obliterated everything."

"I'm not sure we have time for that. You'll see what I mean."

Marcy kept quiet. She would find time.

"Here." Lynde set down a container and a bowl. "You need water and you need to eat. You're part human, after all."

Pain or no pain, Marcy reached for the water. Their hands touched, and she felt renewed warmth flood through her. She reluctantly pulled her hand away, perplexed at this energy within her that was not afraid of this gargantuan Guardian. Hoisting herself on her elbow, she tipped it back and guzzled. So much had happened, she couldn't remember when she last ate. She grabbed the bowl with one hand and brought it to her lips. It was a chunky type of stew, but she didn't see the point in asking for a utensil. Whatever it was satiated her like nothing she'd ever had before. "What is this?"

"I killed a rabbit," Lynde said with a shrug. "I brought supplies with me, too. I had the beans and found some potatoes while you were out."

Marcy set down the emptied bowl. "Days ago, you tried to kill me. Now you're making me rabbit stew?"

Lynde's mouth twitched into a half-grin. "I didn't try to kill you. I merely tried to wake you up. Let's just say that."

Now that Marcy had eaten and drank, the pain had subsided. She sat up slowly. "You experimented with me? All right, I'm intrigued."

"I've been looking a long time for you. Hell is big. Too big. There are billions of creatures and lost souls, not to mention the number of levels. But I heard a rumor in the ranks that there was a Shadow girl different than the others. With abilities, the other Shadow trainees didn't have. I inquired around and practically begged Drakkon to let me do a couple of Guardian shifts watching the trainees. It took me mortal years to find you. When I was sure you had even greater powers that you weren't even tapping into yet, I decided to give you a jumpstart."

Lynde obviously knew more about her than she knew about herself. "Why do I keep not dying?"

"Because you are not who you think you are."

"Who am I?"

Lynde sat up fast and pointed to his lips to keep quiet. He listened, then rolled his eyes and relaxed. "Lover boy ran off when he thought he killed you."

"Lover boy?" Marcy hadn't heard anything. Then something inside the tall brush that surrounded their campfire moved toward them. When Tor stepped out, Marcy didn't hide her disgust. Or her fury. She stood up and glared at him, surprised the pain had already ebbed. He, once again, looked shocked. That only infuriated her more. So, he *had* meant to kill her. *Again.*

The anger mixed with the energy until it exploded from her

hands. She shot him so far so fast that Tor scorched a path through the brush.

"Oh, this ought to be good," Lynde said under his breath.

But Marcy had already begun to run toward Tor. Before she realized what was happening, she had already traveled the distance and tackled him, pinning him between her knees.

Tor took one look at her and exploded into flames, shoving her off of him. In one swift move, she was pinned under him, his sword pointed over her heart.

"Go ahead," she spat at him. "Try it again. We both know you'll *fail.*"

He stared down at her with such contempt and hatred that Marcy was the first to look away.

She could easily throw him off her, what good would it do? Tor beat her hands-down in combat. So, he couldn't kill her. So what? He could still make her life miserable.

Suddenly she felt the pressure lift. Glancing up, she saw Tor had stood up and placed his sword in its sheath. "I'm not going to hurt you this time. That's not my intent. My training is to kill to the death, especially in combat. I've done it so much that instinct took over." He sighed in frustration. "Will you take a walk with me?" he asked without looking at her.

"A walk?" Marcy's mind reeled. "No. Why would I go for a walk with you?" She got up and turned toward the fire and Lynde.

"I promise I won't try to kill you. Doesn't seem to do any good anyway."

"Let me go tell Lynde."

"You don't have to tell him everything. It's just a little walk."

"You told me that a Guardian can disintegrate a Shadow into ash and that Shadows die all the time. I'm not going to upset him by leaving with you."

"That's it though. You can't die, Marcy, and I want to know why."

Marcy sighed and said, "That makes two of us."

18

Human Emotions

There was no one Tor hated more than himself. He tried to rationalize that it was instinct to grab the sword. That she had asked for it. But it had only been *training*. She had got him so worked up with jealousy, that he couldn't even see straight. He had wanted her to choose him. It had given him a sliver of hope he had never experienced. Then she chose Lynde.

But none of that excused his actions. And he knew it. He had no idea how she lived through it. When she had fallen on her face, he had bent down to turn her over, to help her. Until he saw the life gone from those blue eyes of hers. Nothing had ever affected him the way that did. His heart, the one he denied existed, seemed to rip in half. So, he ran. Not only because Lynde would have every right to retaliate and kill him, but because he didn't know how to handle the emotion that needed a release.

And now she was alive again. He came back to report to Lynde. He could have gone straight to Drakkon, who would have been happy that his original plan for Marcy finally worked, but Tor didn't want to. He was glad he had chosen to stay in the mortal realm and check in with Lynde, even though Marcy had glared at him with hatred. Even though she had attacked him again. But this time, at least he put the sword away. He practiced self-control. That was new. And he was starting to understand why. The answer was her.

He glanced over at her. They stood a small brook that ran through the trees. After he ran, he found this place. He had sat here for hours, contemplating, and staring at the sky. He had never stared at the sky before. Not before her. Now he watched as she knelt at the water and proceeded to cup some in her hands and wash her face and neck. She had to move her hair to get to it.

"Are you going to say something?" she asked, as she stood back up. "You asked to go for a walk and haven't talked yet. If this is a trick to lure me away from Lynde, he is not going to be happy."

Too much was happening. He needed to grapple with the emotions, devise a plan, and…There was a blank. It was as if killing her would have ended any kind of future he could foresee for himself. "Just trying to find the right words."

"Finding words has never been a problem for you."

"I…I didn't mean to…"

"Slice me with a sword? Throw me down a never-ending waterfall? Set me on fire?"

"You know what? Forget it." Guardians didn't have to apologize. Had any creature in hell ever said, "I'm sorry?" He doubted it. What had he been thinking? This Shadow girl was the most irritating, infuriating being in all of creation!

He had already begun walking away from her, when he heard her say, "I'm sorry."

That stopped him. Of course, she would apologize. She didn't have a mountain of pride to climb over like he obviously did. And he had been the one to kill her! He groaned out loud. "What is going on in my head?"

"Is your head bothering you?"

He turned back to face her. "Why are you different from every other creature in hell?"

"I don't know. I'm not that different. I can dream weave like other Shadows."

"You don't die."

"Yeah, there's that."

"You seem to be inherently good?"

"Do I? I don't think I am. I've contemplated killing you several times."

"Are you inherently good? Yes, you are, Marcy. Who apologizes in hell? Who hugs Shadow trainees and sacrifices so that a friend doesn't get dumped into an inferno? You do."

"I...I don't know what you want me to say."

"I don't get it," Tor said, as he walked back to her. "You bring things—emotions—out in me that I've buried deep. It's complicated. I used to accept my duties and my lot in life. I never contemplated anything else. Any other existence."

Marcy gave him a look of disbelief. "You've tried to kill me how many times? And now you want me to think that you have conflicted emotions because of me?"

"I don't know what I'm trying to say."

"So, you are done trying to kill me? I'm not sure how I heal from all of your attacks, but it still hurts. A lot."

"I have all these feelings that are new to me. I feel guilty for making you hurt. I think it's guilt. It's a foreign feeling, but it feels bad, and I want to make it right." Tor held his head in his hands. "I don't know what is going on with me."

Lynde shoved into the clearing. "There you are. Make sure to tell me where you're going."

"After I tackled him and we fought some more, he asked me to go for a walk. So, he could tell me he wouldn't try to kill me again."

Lynde looked from Tor to Marcy. "Marcy, can you handle walking back to the camp? I'll be right behind you."

Marcy gave Tor one last look, then said, "Sure."

Lynde kept his steely gaze on Tor. This was it. Tor knew that according to Guardian rules—what few there were—you didn't mess with each other's Shadows. And Tor had done more than that.

"Don't ever raise a hand to hurt her again." Lynde stepped closer to Tor. "And don't ever think about touching her either. I see your thoughts. You wear them openly." Lynde easily looked down at him. "You don't understand the repercussions."

"I get it," Tor spat out. "She's yours. End of story."

"It's not that. She's different."

"I know. I've tried to kill her a couple of times, remember?"

"You're different, too. But not in the same way. It'll become clearer. I promise."

That stopped Tor. "Where is this going?" Lynde had never

spoken to Tor until today. All Tor knew about this massive Guardian was that no one in hell messed with him. Even Drakkon seemed to listen to him. Something about him demanded respect. But Tor still hated him, especially because Marcy chose Lynde over himself.

"But one thing *you're* not," Lynde said, ignoring Tor's comments. "Is indestructible. Do you understand where I'm going with this?"

"I'm not an idiot. If you want to fight right now, let's do it. But stop lecturing me like I'm a child."

Lynde grabbed Tor by the shoulders. "Think about it, Tor. If you were a real demon, a real Guardian, or any spirit being *from* hell, you would not care about Marcy the way you do. You're not from there. You don't belong there."

That ticked Tor off. "Leave me alone, and I'll leave you alone. Got it?" Flames exploded off of him, but Lynde didn't blink. Didn't move a muscle.

"Are you done with your temper tantrum? As I was saying, if you care about her at all, then you have to leave her alone. Drakkon has already figured out that she cares for others. Why do you think that young Shadow trainee was caged too? Drakkon will try to use you to destroy her. Do you understand?"

Tor was just about ready to employ some warrior tactics to get away from Lynde, but his words, once again, stopped him. The truth of what Lynde said hit him straight in the heart; the one spot he had denied ever existed. Could Lynde be right? But Tor already knew the answer.

"That's what Drakkon wants," Tor admitted.

Lynde released him, and Tor walked away, pressing his hands to his head. Drakkon always had a plan to get what he wanted. He knew Marcy was invincible. So, he must have figured to get what he wanted out of Marcy, he would use her one weakness. "Her humanity," Tor said out loud.

"And yours," Lynde said quietly.

Tor turned to him, truly seeing him for the first time. He wondered if Lynde could give him answers to questions he had repressed for years. "I'm not human."

"Yes, you are."

"Drakkon said—"

"We both know Drakkon is a liar. You are a human, and the only reason you have not been killed yet by any of the demons who hate you, by the way, is because there are strict orders not to."

"What?"

"No one can touch you, and it's because you are human. Drakkon doesn't want you dead just yet. He needs your talents."

"If I'm human, why can I do what I do? Do you know about my past?"

"You and Marcy are connected. Not just in your abilities, but also in your past. Your fates are intertwined. Or so that is what was foretold."

"By who?"

Lynde shook his head. "Now's not the time. Too much is

already at stake, but if you want to save both your life and hers, you'll stay away from her."

Tor wasn't satisfied with that answer. Even if he wanted to stay away from Marcy, he wasn't sure he'd be able to. There was something about her energy, whatever was within her, that drew him to her. But Lynde was right. If Drakkon thought that Marcy had a weakness, he'd exploit it, just as he did with Marcy's friend. "Fine, but when I'm done with training her, you better tell me everything."

"Or what?" Lynde didn't act the slightest bit intimidated.

"I tell Drakkon everything you just told me."

Lynde's features hardened. "You won't do that."

"I will. Whatever is going on, I demand answers."

"You don't tell me what to do, Tor. And if you dare go to Drakkon and put Marcy in danger, prophecy or not, I'll kill you myself."

19

Surprise Attack

Tor's words and actions confused her. The walk back might have been long, but Marcy paid no attention. She stayed lost in thought the entire journey back to the fire.

Marcy thought Tor hated her, and she hated him. He tried to kill her at least three times already. The last time was mere hours ago. She could see that Tor was experiencing great discomfort in whatever guilt he felt. Weird. The whole situation was weird.

A part of her wanted him to leave. After her conversation with Lynde, she wanted more of whatever was happening between them. But there would be no chance of that happening because Tor seemed to always be around.

Be careful, the thought popped into her head. *Tor's loyalties are with Drakkon.*

She saw the glow of the fire in the distance and headed toward it, hoping that she and Lynde could continue their conversation privately tonight.

"Where have you been?" His words shot a cold, evil chill up her spine. Rakye hovered over the flames; his face more disgusting than she last remembered. His eyes traveled down her body, holding their gaze just below her waist. Marcy's skin began to crawl. "You still owe me, by the way. So, your Guardian will have to share."

Before Marcy could move, Rakye had leaped for her, holding her in his clutches. She screamed, as his long tongue licked her face. She tried to kick, tried to move her hands, but his power overwhelmed her. So, she screamed for all she was worth.

He had already ripped her shirt. "Yes, scream. Scream loud. It makes it that much more rewarding when I take you."

The energy in her roared, and he flew back into the flames of the fire. He jumped back out and straddled her. "Yes, mortal one, do it again."

This time the attack came from behind. Lynde grabbed Rakye and hurled him far away. Marcy wiped at her eyes and nose, unaware she was sobbing. The screech in the air made her flinch in terror. "Do not be afraid," Lynde said. "What is in you is greater than anything Drakkon can throw at you. Never forget that." Then he was gone.

Lynde had shot right up into the sky. Could Guardians fly? But Marcy was too exposed to think too much about it. She ended up having to turn the shirt around to cover her chest. Something hit something else so hard that the earth seemed to quake from it. Lynde landed right in front of Marcy, and she jumped.

"It's all right," he said. "Rakye is long gone. Let's hope he gets the message and leaves you alone." Still, Lynde stood listening for some time. "We need to travel now. Let me get you a clean shirt." He went to his bag of supplies and brought out a mammoth t-shirt.

"I always have a couple of clean items. It's large, but it'll do better than what you have."

Marcy took the shirt and tried to smile in gratitude but couldn't. Lynde turned around. She pulled the shirt over her head. "Thank you. I'm ready."

She was far from ready. Exhaustion hit her like a freight train. The thought of traveling made her want to fall over, but she wouldn't be able to sleep here. Not after what happened.

Lynde seemed to read her mind. "If Rakye knows where we are, so does every devil in hell. Part of any Shadow's training is the constant onslaught of demons. It's supposed to build strength and courage, but mostly it destroys a Shadow. They either die or start to see things differently. Even though they can't technically kill you, I don't want that for you. You already have too much that needs to be accomplished. It'll be safer if we kept hell guessing where we are. They found us much faster than I anticipated."

"It's hard for me to process that you plan to protect me. A couple of days ago, you were a horrible Guardian who attacked me."

Lynde approached her but kept some distance, which seemed kind. After Rakye's visit, Marcy wasn't ready for any more touching. "I wish I didn't have to do that. The whole grabbing you and instigating an attack. It's not who I am." Lynde paused and listened. "We need to leave."

Marcy helped Lynde dump dirt on the small fire, then she followed him through the tall grass. "Where are we now?" She kept as close to Lynde as possible.

"Ireland. I tried to pick a remote location, but it wasn't remote enough. Then again, they may be tracking us through Tor."

"How far will we travel tonight?"

"I don't know. I'm still working out the details. I've been planning things as we go. This has been a first for me, and I've been around since the beginning."

"Why don't you just extend a blue mist, and we can travel that way."

"Because that would leave a definite trail. That is the best way to connect with a Guardian is through his mist."

"It's like leaving a footprint in hell?"

"Exactly."

Marcy didn't want to ask the question, but it kept plaguing her mind. "What would have happened if Rakye had been successful?"

Lynde stayed quiet long enough that Marcy wondered if he heard her. Then he responded, "Once he's done with you, he devours you. That's how the souls get entrapped inside of him."

"Devours? As in…he eats me?"

"He transforms to a raven and wraps you in his wings, and yes, he swallows you whole." Lynde shuddered. "He represents the great abyss. It doesn't get much eviler than him. Other than Drakkon, of course. I'm not sure what would have happened if he had tried to devour you. You are so powerful that you might have disintegrated him. But without you truly knowing your powers or identity, we can't take any chances."

Marcy hadn't realized she'd slowed down until her skin erupted in goosebumps. Fear gripped her, and she ran to keep up with Lynde, smacking into him. He turned to her and grabbed her wrists. At first, she protested until she saw that he meant no harm. His thumb rubbed the mark on her wrist. "Fear has no place inside of you."

"Then why am I afraid?" She could feel her knees knock, even her teeth chattered and not from any cold.

"Say it: Fear has no place inside me."

Marcy swallowed and repeated, "Fear has no place inside me." She felt the energy respond to the words.

"Again," Lynde encouraged.

"Fear has no place inside me." The words came out stronger, and the energy coursed through her as if the words replenished it.

"When you give in to their tactics, it weakens you. You have to never give in to it. Not to fear. Not to confusion. Not to chaos. As long as you do that, your power will be unmatched."

His words traveled through her like a musical melody that unlocked something buried deep. Everything came together like newly found missing pieces to a puzzle. *Lynde searched to find her. His first and only attack revealed this energy inside of her. He saved her from the inferno. He helped her not sign her name in her own blood. He saved her from Rakye.* "You're not a Guardian," she said. "You're not like any of them. Not even Tor."

Lynde took her hand and ran her fingers along his wrist. She felt the raised teardrop on his skin. Her eyes widened in surprise. "You're like me."

"In many ways, yes." He released her and kept walking.

Marcy rubbed her wrist, still in shock. "Don't leave me hanging! Explain."

"I promise, I will, but not here. We have to get to a safe location. At least a safer location than where we're at."

"What about Tor? Are we trying to hide from him, too?"

"He'll find us. He has his own journey to complete."

"But can we trust him?"

"No, we can't."

"Then let's ditch him. I appreciate that he tried to apologize, but I'm tired of him trying to kill me."

Lynde chuckled. "Even though it's tempting, ditching him is not an option. He needs us."

"He would never admit that."

Lynde chuckled again. "True."

Now that the Rakye incident had settled down in Marcy's mind, she wondered where Tor was. Lynde had been the one to save her, but hadn't Tor heard her screams, too?

Suddenly Lynde stopped. He turned to Marcy; his eyes wide. "Brace yourself."

Marcy felt the cold evil. She turned in a full circle, swallowing down a whimper. "Is he back?"

"Probably not him, but I wouldn't be surprised if it's an onslaught."

"An onslaught of what?"

"Marcy, look at me."

She turned to look at Lynde.

"Don't succumb to the fear. You are greater and more powerful than anything that's going to come at you."

"Can we go somewhere…should we hide…"

Suddenly, Lynde disappeared. As in vaporized in front of Marcy. She covered her mouth to keep her scream in place. *Don't give in to fear. Don't give in to fear.* Chattering filled her ears right before the cockroaches attacked her. She couldn't stop the scream but shut her mouth just as fast as the bugs tried to get in it. They crawled everywhere, biting and chattering. Marcy couldn't swipe them all off. She became angry and desperate at the same time. That's when she felt the energy. She nearly laughed at its welcomed presence. *Get them off of me*! She screamed in her head.

She felt the power push from her body as the nasty cockroaches went flying through the air. They came back in full force but swarmed near her feet unable to touch her.

The shield. She had evoked a shield again. This time she laughed out loud and began stepping on them. Each crunch let out a shriek until eventually they fell back and formed the shape of a man.

"You are not one of us," it hissed.

"No, I'm not. Now leave me alone."

"You must die. You cannot live!"

Marcy's anger pulsed through her body in waves. "I said, 'Leave me alone!'" She outstretched her hands and released the energy from inside her. It blasted the cockroach man, turning him into nothing but a pile of ash.

Her heart pounded, but the energy seemed to tell her not to let down any defenses just yet. For starters, Lynde wasn't back from wherever he disappeared to. Marcy hoped that he would show up with some reasonable explanation for why he disappeared. Secondly, she could hear something—or some*things*—slithering through the grass.

"Please don't be snakes."

Black snakes with glowing red eyes came out from the grass, coiling, and trying to attack her. Their fangs stuck out of their mouths like massive drills ready to take a bite out of Marcy. They kept hissing, "Marcyyyy," before lunging at her.

"A sword or weapon would be useful right now!" she yelled while jumping away from the snakes. The shield still shimmered around her, but with the slithering creatures, it became difficult to concentrate on anything other than them. The sheer number and size of the snakes all moving and lashing out at her had bile rise in her throat. The cockroaches didn't seem nearly as evil and deadly.

She held out her hands to have the energy blast them into oblivion, but a snake—whose head was bigger than hers—jumped up to try and bite it. Shield or no shield, Marcy screamed and dropped her arms. In a panic, she searched around for anything that could help until she refocused her energy. If she had Tor or Lynde's sword, there wouldn't be a problem. "Yeah, leave the girl with the demon snakes and *no weapon*!" she yelled again.

"Marcyyyy," the snakes hissed.

That's when she saw a long stick resting off to the side. If she could just get to it…

She stared at it and willed it to come to her, wondering, hoping, begging for it to work as it had before. Suddenly, the stick flew into her hand. It was much longer and thicker than she had originally supposed, but it would do the job. Marcy simply didn't have time to be surprised.

Nor could she be surprised as she expertly wielded the stick like a sword, attacking the snakes with all the power she could muster. She impaled the snakes, smacked at them, and somehow with a long stick, killed every last snake until ash covered the ground and floated in the air like dark snow from a snow globe.

She panted from the exertion, but she felt good. She listened to see what else would be next. Despite her small victory, she wanted a reprieve from the demons trying to kill her. At least until she could catch her breath. Marcy stared at the stick and wondered. Tor had taught her some basic moves, but some kind of instinct took over when she fought the snakes. There had to have been a couple dozen of them. She had slaughtered them all.

Marcy had a small smile on her face when she heard the movement behind her. Without thinking she spun on her foot wielding the stick for another attack. And stared straight into the eyes of Drakkon.

Lynde and Tor stood at each side, both stared at her in unadulterated shock. Marcy returned her focus to Drakkon. He seemed agitated. "Do you realize how many demons you just killed?!"

"Then they shouldn't have attacked me." Marcy refused to feel guilty when she felt this good.

"It's *training*," Drakkon enunciated the word. "They're *supposed* to attack you."

"And then what? Die?"

"That doesn't seem to be an issue for you, does it?"

"But what about other Shadows?" Marcy thought of Mathilde and shuddered. "Do they get attacked like this? Do they get nearly raped? No wonder they all look so messed up after they join the ranks!"

Drakkon stepped forward. "Silence! You do not talk to me this way. I am your Master. You do things my way, or I will finish what I started in hell."

"Sir, if I may," Lynde stepped forward. "Marcy has shown great promise. Her ego needs adjusting, but I will take care of that, rest assured."

Marcy continued watching Drakkon, not only because Lynde really knew how to sound scary, but also because Drakkon continued watching her with a stony expression on his face. She needed to remember her place or it might not be only her that suffers a horrible fate. And if she'd truly been gifted with everlasting life, then that would make the inferno everlasting torture. So, swallowing her pride, she said, "Sir, I apologize for sounding disrespectful. Please forgive my weariness."

Drakkon gave her a twisted smile. "Forgive you?" He took

another step until his face nearly touched hers. She could smell his sickeningly sweet scent like that of moldy fruit. In her ear, he whispered, "There is no forgiveness in hell. I forget nothing and hold grudges for eternity." Then in a swift move, he grabbed her neck, squeezing the air out of her. "What would happen if I snapped your neck? Would you live? Or maybe I will strangle you."

"Think of her powers, sir." Marcy heard Lynde as she started to black out.

Drakkon released her, and she dropped to her knees, holding her neck and gasping for air. He walked back to the two Guardians and said, "Break her. Do I make myself clear?"

By the time Marcy was able to breathe again, Drakkon had left. Where he went, she didn't know. But he vanished just as Lynde had.

"That was stupid!" Tor yelled. "Do you know what you just did? Drakkon is going to be watching your every move. If you do anything that displeases him, you and anyone else associated with you will be tortured or killed. If you want to keep flirting with the idea that you can't die, that's your own death sentence, but you might want to consider those pathetic trainee friends of yours!"

Marcy had yet to look up at either him or Lynde. Marcy felt the tightness in her chest, and the emotion rise. Tears threatened. "I need a moment."

"No." That was Lynde, but the word was gentle. "We need to keep moving, or it could get even uglier."

"I need a moment. Please."

"Did you hear him? No!" Tor shouted. "You don't tell us or anyone else what to do! You're nothing but a low-life Shadow slave. Now move it." To Lynde, Tor asked, "Are you going to let a Shadow slave tell you what to do?"

The anger burned in her. Burned through to her fingers and toes. On the plus side, her tears had disappeared. "What you need to do," she said in a quiet calm, "is to shut up."

"When are you going to learn that that mouth of yours does nothing but get you in trouble?"

"For the record, I've had to endure being assaulted, a range of demons trying to kill me, and a Guardian who buried his sword into my stomach. Needless to say, my patience factor is below zero."

"That's enough." Lynde held up his hand to Tor. "She's right. She needs to rest." To Marcy, he added, "We do need to leave. I would try to honor your wishes, but we are putting ourselves in more danger, the longer we stay here."

Marcy nodded. Lynde gave her a sympathetic smile, which contrasted with his monstrous form, but she returned the small smile. "After you."

As Lynde led the way, Tor watched Marcy for a second, sighed, then said, "Go ahead. I'll follow behind you."

Without a word, Marcy marched past him to keep up with Lynde.

Tor grabbed her arm. "Marcy…"

Marcy yanked her arm away. "Do not *ever* touch or talk to me again." As she stormed through the long grass to get to Lynde, she pretended not to see the defeat behind his eyes.

20

Purging

It nearly killed him. In more ways than one. But Tor would welcome death at this point. Because *feeling* was killing him. A slow, torturous, miserable death. He tried to take his frustration out on Marcy. Told himself that it was her fault. With her blue eyes, pure energy, and volatile, unpredictable emotions. So many *feelings*, he thought he must be losing his mind.

He remembered what Lynde had said. He understood his reasoning. But asking Tor to practice self-control and stay away from the only female who made his blood boil on so many levels was like asking a starving dog to stay away from a bone.

Tor had stayed back when Lynde left to catch up to Marcy. Needing something cold in a hurry, he dropped his shirt and pants and dunked himself into the brook. He thought the coolness of the brook would bring him to his senses.

That's when he heard her scream.

He stumbled out of the water, throwing dry clothes on a wet body. With his boots back in place, he began to sprint toward Marcy. And ran straight into Drakkon. "Where might you be going?"

Marcy's scream ripped through the forest again. Tor had to

clench his fists and keep a straight face, but he wanted to wrap his hands around Drakkon's neck and snap his head off. If only it were that simple.

"Isn't that a lovely sound? It's the sound of a young, stubborn woman being forced into submission. Alas, her soul will be devoured, but then again, she does crimp our style, doesn't she?"

Tor had to steady his breathing. "She's valuable, sir. If we can bend her will, she'd become your top warrior."

Drakkon glared at him. "You're my top warrior. There is no selflessness around me, so stop acting like a sissy, and do what needs to be done! I wouldn't have to sick Rakye on her if you could control her by now."

"I only met her days ago. You're asking for the impossible."

"No! If it was impossible, Rakye wouldn't be destroying her!" Drakkon shouted, turning into the dragon and lashing out at Tor.

Tor had to think of another tactic. Manipulate. Use Drakkon's methods against him. "Destroy her? Have you seen her power? You know as well as I do, I can't be controlling the weather while fighting on the front lines. I wasn't being selfless; I was thinking smart. Because you taught me that. After she fights with us and helps us win the war, then we destroy her!" Tor made sure to use fire to prove his points because Drakkon responded well to anger. He also responded to flattery.

Drakkon roared before transforming back to the image of a man. "These complications are *trying* my patience. I hate her. There's something about her that riles me up. I was going to stay and watch

Rakye defile her, but I needed to talk to you."

"Why be around that whiny brat any longer than you have to be?"

Now Drakkon smiled, but it was sinister. "Don't think I won't make you pay if you double-cross me."

Suddenly the earth where they were standing shook. Rakye dropped from the sky and into the water, soaking both Drakkon and Tor. The demon pulled himself out of the water, still in bird form. His one wing had been torn off his back and now dangled at his side.

"What happened?" Drakkon seemed in a panic. Almost fearful. "What was it?"

Tor had never seen Rakye so shaken. He wondered if Marcy did this to him and almost smiled.

"A light-bearer…"

"Silence!" Drakkon backhanded Rakye, sending him sprawling into the water again.

Rakye dragged himself out, and fell to his knees, changing to his monster form. His right arm hung limp at his side. "He said our plan would fail."

"If you do not stop speaking, *I* will be the one to rip you apart!"

Rakye seemed to whimper. Tor didn't know whether he should feel disgusted or fascinated. "Can you fix me?" Rakye asked Drakkon, almost sounding like a school child.

"I am not a healer." Drakkon morphed into the dragon and ripped Rakye's arm off the rest of the way.

Rakye screamed and went to lash out. Drakkon roared, grabbing Rakye between his sharp teeth and whipping him across the clearing. Rakye smacked a tree with his enormous body, breaking the tree in half. When he fell to the ground, dark, demon blood spewed from his abdomen. The souls trapped inside of him wailed, creating an eerie moan that made Tor's hair stand on end.

Drakkon turned quickly back to Tor with Rakye's blood still on his teeth and mouth. Once again in human form, Drakkon pulled out a perfectly creased handkerchief from his suit pocket and wiped daintily at his mouth. "Demon blood is not enjoyable."

Tor knew not to react. One time, as an older boy but not yet a teen, he watched Drakkon attack a legion of demons, mutilating them before throwing them in the inferno to burn to death. Tor had tried to be tough, but he must have shown some sort of reaction because Drakkon in his fury threw Tor into isolation for a month. Being in total darkness where the darkness is a real and powerful entity breaks any being, especially a child. But Tor had learned his lesson.

So, he acted nonchalant when he commented, "I'm just glad he's dead."

"He's not. Did he turn to ash? When he comes to, he'll be cranky. And we'll have to reattach his arm. It'll be torturous and absolute agony, so I'll have to make sure and watch."

Tor snuck a glance over at Rakye who had yet to move.

"But I will make it up to him," Drakkon said, tapping his finger to his chin. "Oh yes. I will give him Marcy. Once we have used her powers to destroy all of mankind, Rakye can enjoy her, then devour her, of course. Good thinking, my protégé. Come, let's see how she is doing after a full-scale attack. Even if she lived through him, Rakye was only the start of her eventful night."

Tor felt his stomach roll. Drakkon raised his eyebrow at him as if he heard it. Tor swallowed down the bile. "If they can't kill her, let's hope she's at least broken."

"Broken. Yes, I like that word. Broken. Don't worry, Tor. I will not stop until she is *broken*. Is Lynde with her now?"

Tor hoped so, but he said, "How should I know?"

"I need to talk to him."

Lynde stepped out from behind a tree. "Yes?"

Drakkon jumped, which did not make him happy. "I didn't call for you yet."

"I thought you did. Did you need something? My Shadow is in over her head with a demon."

"So, she's still alive. That's what I wanted to know. Stay here with me. I'm getting annoyed that she won't die."

"Then I will have no Shadow."

"There are millions of Shadow trainees, Lynde. I'm starting to think you wanted that girl to choose you."

"I did," Lynde said without pause. "When I tried to put her in her place during that one training expedition, she had this energy inside of her that she had yet to use or even come to terms with. But I felt that energy. I knew right then that I wanted her as my subject. A Shadow with great talents like that will come in useful to a Guardian."

"Well, too late. She's too much of a risk, and I can't have anything go wrong. I have waited for this day to come when mankind would turn on themselves. They cannot have redemption. They must die. When they die, they become mine. As my army grows, I will be unstoppable. So, pick another trainee because Marcy's time is up." Drakkon extended a mist. "Let's see how she's faring."

Then Tor had almost given himself away. It had been Lynde who touched his arm when Drakkon had grabbed Marcy's neck. Tor had created a fireball in a knee-jerk reaction. That would have been death sentences for all involved. What gave him even greater concern was the idea that Marcy could not die. Continued torture would give Drakkon great pleasure.

Drakkon had already observed her fight the demons. Watched as she annihilated them. Watched as she fought deftly, her movements precise as if she had fought many times before. Tor would have been impressed, but he was too worried.

Then Lynde had spoken, and Drakkon dropped her. That's what made Tor snap at her. Because that's when he knew.

He *wasn't* like Drakkon.

He *could* feel.

He *could* love.

But would it save either of them from a fate destined for destruction?

Tor's thoughts came into focus as Marcy tripped and stumbled to the ground. Tor took a step to help, but she held up her hand. "Don't even think about it."

Exhaustion lined her face. Once again, Tor's heart felt an ache.

"How far are we going?" he called out to Lynde. "I think she's had enough for a night."

"I don't need you defending me." She stood up and headed for Lynde, who had stopped to wait. "I'm fine. Keep going."

"No, you're not fine," Tor argued. "Don't be so stubborn that you make stupid decisions."

"Why don't you shut up?" Marcy said, "I never asked you for your opinion. Lynde is my Guardian, not you. So, lay off."

A quick comeback was on his tongue, but arguing with her would only make her more exhausted. Fine. She wanted him quiet? He wouldn't talk. He stepped around her and kept walking. He had gone quite far ahead before he heard Lynde call out to him, "We're here! You passed it."

Tor thought about leaving them behind. Everything had been fine until a couple of days ago. Why did he need to train her? She didn't even need training. Any being—mortal or spirit—who could slay a couple dozen demons didn't need training. That would be best, he resolved in himself. Leave her with Lynde. She decided on someone else as her Guardian. End of story. As long as she existed, she was tied to Lynde. If he severed ties, all the crazy, tumultuous feelings would go away.

Tor stopped in his tracks. Was that what he wanted?

Marcy had been the first spark of anything that Tor had felt for or cared about. What had it been like before her? Did he really want that?

His insides toiled in agony. He held his stomach and tried to breathe in deep breaths. That only made the nausea worse.

Tor had to stop lying to himself. He couldn't think about existence without Marcy in it. When he had to watch her over the inferno, he wanted to die right there. When he had reacted in their training fight, and he had put a sword through her, it was as if someone had reached into his chest and ripped out his heart. But it stemmed from even more than that.

He revolted against the idea of being Drakkon's slave any longer. And that's what he was. He and every other monster in hell were slaves to Drakkon. If it meant dying, then it was better than living under tyranny and evil. He had no idea how to escape the clutches of the dark lord, but there had to be a way. For whatever reason, he started to believe that Marcy may be the key to that escape.

He turned around and walked back to them. They were directly under a massive oak tree, removing tree branches and debris from what looked to be an old, outdated, rusty truck. "There she is," Lynde said wiping the rest of the branches and leaves off of it. "How's my girl?"

"How old is this thing?" Marcy asked.

"Since Drakkon tried to eradicate mankind with the extinction of the chosen people. Here. Help me."

Tor felt a jolt inside that seemed to freeze him in place. For whatever reason his heart beat wildly, a sheen of sweat covered his face, and he felt nausea rise inside his gut.

Lynde said, "Go, get sick, man. We'll wait for you."

Marcy looked up with poorly masked concern.

"What's happening?" Tor asked as his stomach rolled.

"You're purging your system. If you throw up, it'll make you feel better."

Tor opened his mouth to say something, but the bile rose quickly. He ran back to the brush and vomited what little he had in his stomach. Soot and ash also came out, smelling vile. Since he inhabited hell, he had to eat on earth and drink the water to nourish himself, but he never stayed for long. Oftentimes, Drakkon would send minions to do the bidding of finding food for Tor. He had never thought about it much then, but now the thought did not escape his mind that no one else in hell had that same need.

He wiped at his mouth and heard Marcy whisper to Lynde, "Will he be all right?" The concern in her voice made him feel weak. He hated feeling weak. *But at least she cares for you.*

The shudder ran through him fiercely, and he purged again.

The truck started but ran idly while Tor cleaned up.

"Here," Marcy said from behind him.

He turned and saw her holding a canteen of water. "I don't deserve you being kind."

"I'm not being kind. Lynde told me to give it to you." She walked back to the truck and slid into the passenger seat.

Tor would have reached out to touch her again, but he suspected that leaving her alone like Lynde said might be for the best. He didn't know how long he could hold out, but for her safety, he had to try. He rinsed his mouth and sipped some water, finding it went down easy despite just getting sick. After he had wet his face and hair, he walked over to the truck. "Where are you going? I'm supposed to train Marcy, not go for a drive."

"Get in."

"I'll take the back. I need the fresh air."

"I thought you didn't like earth," Marcy mumbled under her breath.

"Suit yourself," Lynde said. "But let's go. Time's wasting."

Tor hopped in the bed of the truck and sat behind Lynde. That way Marcy could stay in his view. He would have liked nothing better than to sit so close to her, but she would have been just as close to Lynde, and nothing like a third wheel to make someone feel included. But more than that, Tor didn't want them to see how shaken he was.

Lynde followed a dirt path with no lights on for what would be an hour in the mortal realm. Marcy had long been sleeping, her legs pulled up beside her, her head leaning against Lynde's shoulder. Lynde had given her an ugly green army blanket to cover her. Now he pulled up the blanket, letting his arm drape around her, holding the blanket in place.

Lynde glanced into the rearview mirror, and they made eye contact. Lynde's arm tightened around her.

The simple gesture started a firestorm inside Tor. He wanted to rip the back window off so that it no longer separated him. Lynde had some affections he wasn't sharing. There was something to Lynde. He'd have to figure it out. And make sure he stayed away from Marcy.

Because if Tor couldn't have her, nobody could.

21

Third Wheel

When Tor opened his eyes, he immediately sat up ready to strike. Then he realized he still sat in the back of the truck, so he extinguished his fire.

Lynde opened up the back sliding window. "Be careful with that fire. Human vehicles have highly flammable gasoline."

Tor rolled his eyes. This know-it-all was the last thing he wanted to wake up to. "Yes, Lynde. I'm not stupid. We also control the fire element, so I'm not too worried." Tor saw Marcy's head now rested on his lap. That burned hotter than hell. "You enjoying yourself?"

"She's *sleeping*. And no, I'm not enjoying myself because while you two have been sleeping for the last ten hours, I've been driving. So, stop grating on my nerves."

"Ten mortal hours?" Tor had never slept that long. In hell, he constantly had to watch his back, so sleeping in short increments served him well.

"Your body must have needed it."

"I handle myself just fine without sleep."

"Newsflash: you're in the mortal realm. Your body is going to change to acclimate to it."

"You know what? I don't want an encyclopedia read-through."

Tor did a quick survey of the landscape. Now that he had slept, he realized how much of a third wheel he was.

"Marcy woke up a couple of times, mostly when I had to stop to fill up. But you've been like the dead."

"When are we stopping?" He glanced around and saw they were driving along some country road that could barely squeeze two vehicles side-by-side. The gray, overcast sky hung heavily, but it fit his mood.

"We're almost there."

"There where?"

"None of your business."

"Hiding from Drakkon is pointless. Trust me, I've tried." Tor stopped himself again. This vulnerability stuff needed to be monitored. He refused to have this big Guardian feel pity toward him. If he even was a Guardian. But if he wasn't, then Tor had no idea who he was. For that reason alone, Tor would need to grit his teeth and bear it.

"The idea is to slow him and the other demons down. Marcy needs her rest. Plus, she needs to complete her training."

"I think she's got skills she hasn't told us about."

"I'm not talking about the kind of training you want to give her. This is different."

Tor couldn't help himself. He asked, "How different?"

Lynde didn't respond.

"Then what am I doing here? I have other things to do!"

"You want to leave? Then leave. Nobody's keeping you with

us. You're the one who turned around last night and came back. A couple of times for that matter." Glancing in the rearview mirror, Lynde said, "I think we both know why you're sticking around."

"One word: Drakkon. I have a job to do. I'll do it, then I will be all too happy to leave." Tor had to throw one last jab in. "We both know you're not a Guardian. At least not one of hell's Guardians. You're way too protective of your Shadow."

"And you wouldn't be? I don't have to explain myself to you. Marcy and I are none of your concern. Do the job Drakkon ordered you to do, then leave us to do what we've been commissioned to do."

Tor could feel the fire in his bones. Not just because Lynde dismissed him, but because of what he said about being commissioned to do something. That meant Drakkon had a task for them that he didn't let Tor in on. He almost jumped off the truck right there, but Marcy sat up and rubbed her eyes. "What's with all the shouting?"

Tor had a quick comeback, but it was stopped short when an enormous being dropped from the sky and stood on the road facing them. Lynde didn't act surprised but slammed on the brakes, throwing Tor against the window.

It slowly approached the vehicle. Tor watched fascinated at the winged man. It had three sets of wings of gold so bright that Tor couldn't look at it for long. His long, translucent hair hung in waves, his chest bearing a solid gold breastplate, his sword almost as tall as he was, completely of gold. Tor felt the violent urge to purge again, but he stayed riveted to this enormous man-creature approaching the vehicle. "You cannot pass." His words held a power to them that made Tor want to hide. He was not a wimp, not by any sense of the word, but he had never—not with all the monsters in hell—experienced a creature that he felt would obliterate him with ease.

"I have access."

"Not in your current state you do not. Light cannot mix with darkness." The creature turned his eyes on Tor.

"She has to be protected."

"She already is."

"Not from everything, and you know it."

"You cannot pass." The man-creature walked to the front of the vehicle and drew his sword. With a flick of his other hand, he turned the entire truck around. That left Tor completely exposed to it. "Light cannot mix with darkness," he said directly to Tor and extended the sword to where the tip of it came to Tor's chest.

Tor couldn't move. All he could do was stare at this fierce creature completely mesmerized. He wondered what death would feel like, but he also had already come to an understanding that dying by this creature's sword would be much better than dying in Drakkon's charge.

"You have been weighed in the balances," the deep voice of the creature said to Tor, "and are found wanting."

It sounded like a curse of some sort, and Tor understood that the charge meant guilt.

Lynde put the truck into gear and took off in the direction they had come from.

"What was that?" Marcy said with fear in her voice. Tor was glad that he wasn't the only one who was intimidated by that thing.

"We've got a problem," Lynde said. "I can maybe get you through another route, but they won't accept Tor."

"Do we at least have the demons off our tail?" Marcy asked.

"They're looking for us. I feel it. You're not done with training, and part of being trained for a Shadow is being broken. Right, Tor?" Lynde asked the question with some anger in the words.

Tor didn't glance at them. He kept his face stone.

"I have to be broken?" Tor heard Marcy's voice turn toward him, but he wouldn't look at her. He remembered his conversation with Drakkon. He had said all of it only to give him more time with her. Now he saw that their future was doomed any way he looked at it. "Tor, if you know something about another attack, it would be nice to know."

The plea in her words made him turn to look at her. Drakkon expected loyalty from him. He warned Tor not to double-cross him, but Tor was tired of Drakkon's orders. "Drakkon means to destroy you."

"But I can't die, right?"

"Destroying a soul is not death. It's everlasting bondage. That's an even worse fate." Tor turned away because seeing the despair in her eyes was too much, and he wondered if she would see the despair in his own eyes.

They drove in silence, which was fine because Tor needed to contemplate his next move. He should probably leave. What would be the outcome of sticking around? Either these feelings would only grow, which would lead to torture when Drakkon had his way with Marcy, or he would sit around as the third wheel watching Lynde and Marcy do whatever they were going to do. The fact that Drakkon had a secret with Lynde grated on Tor's nerves. And that creature. What had it said? "I've been weighed in the balances…" Tor said the words and shook his head.

"Stop here," Marcy said.

Lynde pulled over to a tiny gas station.

"I need to freshen up and get some food. You guys want anything?"

"Yeah," Tor said before he could stop himself. But his stomach kept growling since he woke up. That was a strange feeling. If Lynde was right, Tor needed to eat more mortal food.

"Please?" Marcy prompted.

"I can go in and get it myself." Tor made sure flames came off his hand to prove his point.

"All I'm asking you to do is be polite," Marcy snapped. "You don't have to be so ugly." She got out of the truck and slammed the door. She walked to the side of the building to where the restrooms were.

Tor jumped off the truck.

"I wouldn't be starting any fires." Lynde had stepped out of the truck, as well.

"When are you going to learn that you don't order me around? I'm going to relieve myself if that's all right with you."

Tor walked around the side of the building to the men's restroom. A man stepped out and held the door open for him. Tor blinked in surprise. The mortal could see him? He shut the door behind him and went to the sink. He felt like death. Tor laughed at the thought. "Death. How clever." Still, he washed his face and did the best he could with cleaning up. He looked at the dirty shirt and longed for another one to change into. Someone knocked at the door.

"Tor?"

He opened it up to find Marcy standing there with a pile of clothes in her arms. And she was staring at him. It was then he realized that he was nearly naked.

"Did you steal these?"

She shrugged. "There's a small store across the street. I didn't want to wear Lynde's shirt forever."

Tor took a deep breath. "About what happened with Rakye, I'm not supposed to interfere."

"That's it? *I'm not supposed to interfere?* So, you're fine with these demons attacking me and destroying me?"

"Why are you asking me this? It's complicated, Marcy."

"Because I'm trying to figure out the real Tor. Is it the guy who's tried to kill me? The guy who's sworn allegiance to the evilest being ever? Or is it the guy who asked me to go for a walk and admitted to feelings?"

They stared at each other, but neither moved. "I don't know," Tor eventually said. "I don't know a lot of things. Like who you really are. Like who is Lynde, and why is he so protective of you? I mean, Guardians couldn't care less about their Shadow slaves, but it's different with him."

"I'm glad he's different." Marcy shoved some clothes with tags at Tor. "Here., I had to guess at your size." She turned to walk away. This time he grabbed her.

She went to pull away, but he kept his grip firm. "Marcy, listen."

"What?"

How could he explain? How could he tell her? He *had* sworn allegiance to Drakkon, but as a boy, not as a man. How could he say that he didn't want to hurt her anymore, but that his insides were torn at what to do? How could he say any of this? "Thank you," he said. "For the clothes." He released her and shut the restroom door again.

Tor finished washing up, then changed into the clothes. He studied himself in the mirror. Odd. Now that he thought about it, Guardians didn't have a reflection in a mortal mirror. They were entirely spirit beings. But he could see himself. His chest pulled at the snug t-shirt. His shoulders and arms were also quite defined. Long torso. Long arms. Long legs. He held up his hands. Long fingers. And he was tall. Very tall. It seemed like he was staring at a stranger. Reflections weren't too important, so he rarely saw his. He leaned forward and studied his face. His dark eyes glowed from the fire within.

Standing straight again, he brought fire to his fingertips. He'd have to be careful. The clothing from hell had been engineered to be fire-resistant. This cheap human fabric would disintegrate in seconds.

He stepped out of the bathroom and found Lynde and the truck behind the gas station. "Are we hiding?"

Lynde leaned against his door, staring up into the sky. "Marcy insists on using her Shadow skills to *borrow* some things." Lynde glanced at Tor, then raised his eyebrows. "White t-shirt and blue jeans?"

"With my sword, of course."

"Like that doesn't stand out. You know people can see you, right?"

"Yeah, what's up with that? I thought Guardians were invisible to the mortal's naked eye."

"Tor, it gets tiring having to spell everything out for you."

Tor felt slapped. He felt the heat rising within him. "Do not ever talk to me that way. Ever."

"Then don't make me explain everything. It's not my job to hold your hand."

Tor threw a row of expletives at him, telling him exactly what he could do with himself. He noticed Marcy step out of the shadow that the truck made, but he wasn't going to look away. He'd had enough with this jerk. "Insult me one more time. I dare you." Tor had his hand on his sword.

"You don't want to fight me," Lynde said quietly.

"I think I really do."

"Tor, what happened?" Marcy asked.

"Right. You're asking me because Lynde can do no wrong?"

"That's not what I meant. Your clothes…"

Tor glanced down and noticed the entire outfit had disintegrated. And he was completely naked. Tor positioned one hand to cover his assets while grabbing his pile of dirty clothes. "Don't ever give me human clothes again."

Marcy stared in shock for another few seconds before laughing so hard she had to hold her stomach.

Lynde started to laugh.

Tor walked backward to the restroom, silently cursing human clothing.

22

In the Dark

Lynde took a sharp turn down another narrow country road. Tor sat huddled in the back of the truck, sullen, confused, and parched. This stupid expedition—or whatever it was—confused him more than he wanted to admit. And that made him sullen. Well, plus he wanted to pummel Lynde to a bloody pulp, but that would be stating the obvious.

Beyond all of that, his mouth felt like the desert. He realized being in the mortal realm too long would do bizarre things to him, but he hadn't experienced thirst like this before. He eyed Marcy sipping from a water bottle and made himself not ask for any. That would look vulnerable, and he'd had enough of that.

Marcy turned suddenly, making eye contact with Tor. He looked away, but it was too late. She had spotted him watching her. She grabbed one of the bags she had stolen from the gas station and rummaged through it. Opening up the back window, she asked, "Do you get hungry or thirsty? I have food."

His thirst became greater than his pride. "Water."

Marcy handed him a large water bottle. He opened it and couldn't gulp it fast enough. It tasted amazing. The coolness of the liquid seemed to run like a river through his insides. After he had downed the last drop, he noticed Lynde saying something to Marcy in a hushed tone. She glanced back at Tor guiltily when she saw their conversation had been caught.

"What?" he demanded, losing his cool. When neither one said anything, he stood up, closed his eyes, and stepped off the truck. When he opened his eyes, his fire blazed as he stood on the road in its path.

Lynde slammed on the brakes, fishtailing through the dirt and gravel, and came to a halt directly before Tor.

"What's with all the secrets? And don't give me any of this, 'I don't want to explain it to you' garbage. You are not following protocol at all. You're driving us around in some manmade vehicle, taking us to who-knows-where, and you act like I'm supposed to figure this out. Tell me what's going on before I go back to Drakkon and tell him exactly where you are."

In a blink of an eye, Lynde disappeared from the seat and appeared to Tor's right. "You'll tell him nothing."

Tor expected Lynde's fist and stopped it with his palm. He went to deliver a blow to Lynde's gut, but Lynde stopped him and with super strength threw Tor up in the air. Tor stayed calm, telling himself this was a fight he must win, and he teleported himself directly behind where Lynde stood. Lynde turned, but this time wasn't fast enough. Tor put everything he had into a punch that sent the jerk through the air, as well.

"Guys, stop it!"

Tor heard Marcy, but his adrenaline spoke louder.

"No teleporting!" Lynde bellowed, teleporting himself back to Tor. "If we fight, we fight fair."

Tor teleported directly to Lynde's right and sucker-punched him in the gut. "Guess what? I don't do fair."

Lynde brought his elbow to Tor's chin, and Tor clumsily stepped back seeing stars. Then Lynde hit him again across the face. Tor teleported away from him until he could get his bearings. He heard Lynde shout, "No teleporting, you sissy!"

Tor showed himself right in front of Lynde and tackled him to the ground.

They tumbled and threw punches, throwing each other off, only to step back into the fight. Suddenly, Tor felt an energy pick him up and smash him against a tree so hard, it stole the air right out of him.

"You two boneheads are starting a massive forest fire!"

Marcy hovered over him. He heard Lynde stand to his feet. "This complicates things," Lynde sighed.

Tor forced himself to stand and not act shaken. One glance at Lynde, and he smugly gave himself a mental pat on the back. The Guardian might be tough, but Tor held his own. That's when Tor heard the roaring of flames and the snapping of trees.

Marcy was panicking. Tor puffed himself up, knowing what would impress her. "Watch this," he said. He felt the energy immediately. Normally, he handled larger-scale weather patterns, especially hurricanes and tornadoes, but within seconds he summoned heavy clouds and felt the sheets of rain soaking him.

"You said you controlled parts of the weather. I didn't believe you." Marcy watched in awe.

"Just another way I'm different," he said, watching the rain drench the forest. He had often wondered why he had this gift. Sure, he was tough and skilled and controlled fire like other Guardians. But no one, not even Drakkon himself, could control the mortal's atmospheric storm systems.

"Too bad you're such a putz," Lynde said under his breath.

"Want to say that again, big guy? I can make your other eye swollen."

Lynde faced him and asked, "What are you talking about?"

Tor noticed the injuries Lynde had sustained had disappeared. He looked just as ugly as before.

"Just another way I'm different," Lynde said with a smirk.

"If you two do not get a grip, I will whip you like I did those demon snakes."

Tor and Lynde turned to her. "Yeah, how'd you do that?" Tor asked. They all stood in the rain, but none of them made their way to the truck. "I hadn't shown you any of those moves."

"I don't know," she said with a shrug. "But I'm sure if I did it once, I can do it again. So, don't mess with me. Or each other."

"Then let's get some things straight," Tor said to the both of them. "I'm here because I was assigned to be here. I'm here to train Marcy. Not go on some stupid mortal adventure. So, when I ask, 'Where are we going?' or 'What are we doing?' I would like a response."

"I gave you a response," Lynde said through gritted teeth. "You need to get this through your thick, hell-damaged skull. *I* am Marcy's Guardian. Everything I am doing is for her training. Right now, I want her at her best. Being attacked by a deluge of demons, including you, has worn her down. So, I'm using manmade materials and trying to find a refuge for us for a while. There. Are you satisfied?"

"Why are you acting more like her protector, than her Guardian? I've never met a Guardian who gave one thought about their Shadow. I don't trust it, and I don't trust you."

"And what would have happened if she had picked you, huh? Would you have let those demons defile her? Kill her? Rob her soul?"

"N-N-o," Tor stumbled over the words. What would he have done if Marcy had chosen him?

"What would you have done, Tor?" Marcy asked quietly. "You didn't do anything when Drakkon was about to snap my neck. Lynde stepped up. And Lynde was there to throw Rakye off of me. Where were you?"

"What do you want me to say? I don't know about anything anymore. I don't know who I am or where I came from or how I even got to be in hell in the first place! But some rules have to be followed to survive. And this little adventure we're on is going to get somebody killed. Mark my words."

Lynde said quickly, "Stop the rain and let's get going. The forest will be fine. And if it'll make you feel more like a man or Guardian or whatever you want to call yourself, go march to Drakkon and tattle like a little five-year-old twerp."

As Lynde headed for the truck, Tor noticed Marcy not moving. "Do you want to go back to Drakkon?"

Tor looked into her eyes and in a moment of honesty said, "No. I don't know what's going on with me, but I do know that it took every ounce of willpower not to attack him when he had his hand around your throat."

"You could have tried."

"Don't you get it, Marcy? It would have ended horribly. Human empathy gets you and those you care about killed. I don't want either one of us to be dead."

"Stop the rain!" Lynde shouted from the truck.

Tor closed his eyes, inhaled deeply, and allowed the energy to create a light wind to dissipate the clouds. He felt the warmth of the sun's rays break through and felt himself smile again.

"It's nice, isn't it?" Marcy said. "The mortal realm is amazing. This is the longest I've been in it, and I don't know. It feels like I've never left."

He peeked over at her and saw her face inclined toward the sun.

"Parts of it, but I've mostly seen all the dark parts of the mortal realm. I've never enjoyed the sun before."

"Waiting!" Lynde yelled.

Tor glanced over at the truck and sighed, "I don't like that guy."

"I do." Marcy made eye contact with Lynde, and Tor observed their shared smile. "He's not bad, and you know it. I should have been broken by now, remember? And he's the one who's protected me on more than one occasion."

Tor tried not to show any jealousy. "Yeah, well, I don't trust him. Or like him." He walked toward the truck.

He and Lynde exchanged measured glances.

He took one look at the back of the truck and sighed again. None of this still made any sense, but he wouldn't go back to Drakkon. He already tried to avoid any thought about when that moment would happen. The very core of him knew that Drakkon wasn't about to let his top warrior and this gifted Shadow just ramble around the mortal realm. He probably was already in hot pursuit. That sent a cold shiver through Tor.

"Hey," Marcy said through the open back window. "What we had been discussing before you went all nuts is that you're probably hungry, too. Do you want something to eat? I snagged some burritos and chips, along with the water." She dug through a bag again and produced a now lukewarm burrito, a bag of potato chips, and another bottle of water.

Tor's stomach grumbled in response. He took them and nodded in appreciation.

"What was that?" Marcy asked him. "Was that a *thank you*?"

He gave her a lop-sided grin. "Thank you."

Marcy covered her mouth in apparent shock. "Wonder of wonders."

"Shut up," he said as he guzzled the second bottle of water. "I've never needed water this much." He took a bite of the extra grande bean burrito and nearly groaned in pleasure. "What's in this?"

"Beans, cheese, and onions wrapped in a tortilla shell," Marcy said with a shrug. "The trainees love them."

"And enough chemicals to put hair on your chest," Lynde said without looking up from the road.

"You can't get this in hell," Tor said between mouthfuls.

After the wave of volatility and a stomach full of food, Tor found himself dozing again.

The sound woke him up. He lifted his head, which had been resting on his knees, and listened. Tor heard the crash of the waves against the rocks and without thinking, drew in a deep breath of fresh, salty sea air. And he froze.

A memory scraped at the corners of his mind. Salty air. He closed his eyes and concentrated. What was it?

"What's that?" Marcy asked.

Tor looked and saw a small Irish abbey sitting on a cliff. It seemed out of place with the lush greenery that surrounded it and the sound of waves crashing below it, yet something about it seemed familiar.

Lynde made a sharp turn, driving down a narrow path into a dense canopy of forest. Tor hoped it wasn't like the other place Lynde drove them to, but curiosity had him scrutinizing the landscape. Something non-mortal dwelled here. Tor felt the energy inside of himself hum in response to the palpable sensation of the supernatural that hung like a fog in the air.

Okay, so this was *a lot* like the place Lynde had taken them with the bizarre winged creature. Just thinking about what the creature said to Tor brought an uneasiness to his being. Whatever this supernatural aura was, it might be hostile to Tor.

The bearers of light would be hostile. They were the only other supernatural entities. Soldiers of the Nameless One. Drakkon's sworn enemies. Protectors of mankind. Hell's captors. Realization hit Tor like an arrow slicing its target.

Lynde.

The creature addressed Lynde as if they knew each other. Lynde tried to access whatever place that was. He mentioned something about protecting Marcy.

Could they be light-bearers? Tor mentally shook himself. They couldn't be. Lynde was one of the ugliest Guardians Tor had ever encountered. And his scars. Not to mention he controlled fire and could access the realms. Beyond that, it wasn't possible to be inhabitants of hell and soldiers of the Nameless One. Those two worlds could not collide. At least not yet. Tor knew that if Drakkon's overall plan worked, they would be tearing down the celestial gates and overtaking the Master Throne. Drakkon had told Tor once that he would sit at the throne beside him. The prince of the new world order.

The truck came to a stop at a running river with large rock monuments on both sides. Tor wondered what had once stood here.

Lynde turned around. "This is your stop."

Tor blinked. "What? Is this where we train?"

"Yes. Marcy and I will camp elsewhere. Not too far from here.

We will meet you here at daybreak." Lynde pointed at one of the towering rock columns. "Just past these ruins is a cave that miners used when searching for minerals back in the day. I've stayed there before. Please understand that this place is safe. As long as you stay within the protected boundaries, Drakkon cannot get to you."

Tor looked from Lynde to Marcy and knew that he had no place beside them, other than to fulfill Drakkon's orders of training her. But the thought of being protected from Drakkon relieved Tor more than he wanted to admit. "How am I supposed to train her in every aspect of hell's war tactics if we can't go back to hell?"

"We're not going to hell for a while yet. I'm only asking for some time so that Marcy can get her strength back. Once you've trained her in your tactics, and I've trained her in mine, she'll be much more equipped to handle the onslaught that's coming."

Marcy eyed Lynde warily. Tor saw the fear flash on her countenance. Unfortunately, he knew Lynde was right. He jumped out of the truck, ready for some time alone to concentrate and figure out his plan.

Because one thing was certain, Tor would figure out what was going on. He had had enough of being in the dark. He had had enough of being someone else's pawn. And he was finally in a place where he would have some time to think without the fear of being caught. Not that he was about to say thank you. "See you at daybreak," he said over his shoulder as he walked in the direction of the ruins.

23

The Truth

Marcy snuck a glance out the side view mirror and watched Tor walk away.

"He'll be fine," Lynde said, as he put the truck in drive and inched along the path.

"I'm sure he will be," she said, keeping her eyes on Tor's retreating figure.

"You need to be careful, Marcy."

"Why's that? Other than the obvious, of course."

"I'm talking about Tor. He's struggling with loyalties right now. I'm not going to lie and say he doesn't have feelings for you. He does. But he gave a sworn oath to Drakkon, and if push came to shove, I'm not sure we can trust him."

Marcy studied Lynde. "I'm not too sure about Tor having feelings toward me. He has tried to kill me quite a few times."

"The longer he stays in the mortal realm, the more of his humanity comes to the surface. That means human emotions and feelings. He is drawn to your energy. Who wouldn't be?" Lynde glanced at her and grinned.

"The energy inside of me? Interesting. It feels like it has a mind of its own. What is it exactly?"

"The purest light imaginable." Lynde gave her another small smile. "You know what, you're about to find out."

The forest thinned, and they were back onto a dirt road, leading toward the abbey. Marcy noticed four Celtic crosses atop tall stone pillars set apart at each of the four corners of the abbey's cultivated yard. Marcy and other Shadow trainees were ordered to stay clear from any type of religious posts, and they had to steer clear of human memories that contained religious information. Not that Marcy obeyed.

So, she knew enough to know that this place would be sacred to mortals' worship of the Nameless One. Which meant she and Lynde shouldn't be entering.

"I think you can start answering questions, Lynde."

"Let's see what you already know."

"I know you're not a Guardian."

"But I am."

"Not in hell's sense, you're not."

Lynde made a face. "True."

Just him admitting that brought her a sense of terror and relief at the same time. "I know that we're similar because we bear the same mark."

Lynde made another impressed face. "True."

"How similar?"

He smiled as he drove past one of the Celtic cross pillars. Marcy's energy jolted through her as if being plugged into a supercharger. "Whoa."

"Yeah."

She felt an amazing sensation of power and light and electrified air. "What is this place?"

"It's a portal that connects two worlds. It's very powerful, and no creature of hell can access it."

Marcy turned to look at Lynde in wonder and froze. His appearance had completely transformed. He still had the long, jet-black hair pulled back, but the scars and hellish countenance had been completely erased. It was his face still but different. Very different. She would never have used the word handsome to describe Lynde. Until now. "You look…your face…what…?"

"Look at yourself." He pulled down the old visor that had an oval mirror wrapped around it.

Marcy stared at herself wide-eyed. Her countenance *glowed.* Her blue eyes especially shone brightly like beacons through a fog. It was her face, but somehow her aura had shifted.

"Light and darkness cannot mix. That's why we couldn't access the other sacred grounds. I knew that mortals could not enter there, and with your and Tor's current conditions, you are part mortal, but I wanted to try. Plus, I thought it might spark some memory."

"With Tor? Or with me?"

"With you."

"I've been there before?"

"You were the one who oversaw it."

Lynde pulled up to a side entrance of the abbey while Marcy laughed. She laughed because he acted so seriously. "I hate to break it to you, but you're thinking of the wrong girl."

Lynde opened the door and slid out. Winking at her, he said, "I don't think so."

Marcy gave herself one more glance in the mirror, then quickly closed the visor. All of this new information and sensory experience might have felt overwhelming, but it also felt wonderfully good. She slid out of the truck and shut the door right as a priest and a delivery driver stepped out of the abbey.

"Michael," the priest said in relief. "It was a success." His Irish lilt was lyrical, and his red hair and beard were both big and bushy, but he was so short, that he had to stand on his toes to greet Lynde with a kiss on each cheek. He waved off the driver, who slid back into his truck and backed away. "Levi just brought more supplies. If I would have known you were coming, Michael, I would have ordered more."

Marcy wanted to correct the name he called Lynde, but the priest had already turned to her. His green eyes welled with tears. "I don't know what to say," he said. "I never thought I'd see you again." He grabbed Marcy and embraced her, sobbing into her shoulder.

She looked over at Lynde with a what-in-the-world-is-happening question on her face.

Lynde said, "Timothy, she doesn't remember."

The priest—Timothy—released her, shock on his handsome face. "You don't remember anything at all?"

Marcy glanced from him to Lynde. Something about the man

did seem familiar, but Marcy didn't trust herself at the moment. "Uh, I know that churches are representative of the Nameless One, and I'm supposed to stay away. Not that I want to, but that's what I've been told."

Timothy stepped back almost as if he'd been electrocuted by her words.

"Give her time," Lynde said quietly. "At least I got her out."

Timothy gave a faltering smile. "Of course. Well, I'm Timothy, and I can't tell you how relieved I am that you're here. Are you hungry? Thirsty? Do you need to clean up? Take a nap?"

Marcy smiled. She liked this guy. "Yes, to all of the above."

Now his smile spread across his face. "I am here at your service. Please follow me. Did you bring anything?"

Marcy held up the plastic bag stuffed with a few clothing items she stole from the small retail store across from the gas station. "Just this."

"I have some toiletries and things that you will find useful."

"Thank you."

He motioned for her and Lynde to follow him. Marcy grabbed Lynde's elbow. "Michael?"

"That's my real name."

"Michael?"

"Yes."

"Are you a soldier of the Nameless One?" Marcy's words contained her surprise. "How did you mask it in hell?"

"I'm not a soldier. I'm Master Warrior of the Lord of hosts. And

I was able to mask it in hell, in similar ways that you were able to mask your identity."

"Say what?"

"She doesn't remember, does she?" Timothy now stood between them.

"She will," Lynde—or Michael—said with confidence.

Marcy's head spun. This was what she wanted, wasn't it? To find out why she was different. But she also knew she was part mortal. "Complicated," she said, shaking her head. "This is all so complicated."

"Let's eat and rest," Timothy said, gently taking her arm. "In due time, everything will work itself out. It always does."

Once inside, Timothy led her up a flight of stairs to a partial floor with one room located on it. "This was where you would stay before you left." Timothy seemed to hold his breath as Marcy entered it.

It housed a narrow bed with a small couch and table on the other side. A large desk fit right underneath the opened window that currently let in the strong ocean breeze.

"Those cabinets contain a variety of toiletries and towels, and that adjacent door is your small restroom. We, as in the men, will be down in the priest quarters on the other side of the abbey. Just take these stairs down, and walk across the kitchen area to the back doors. There you will see a set of apartments." Timothy took one more look at her and shook his head. "For what it's worth—even if you don't remember—I'm so glad you've returned." He kissed her cheek and left her standing in the loft-like room.

Marcy sank onto the couch, letting all the events finally take their toll. From fighting off demons to the confusing situation with Tor, to now this new information that she was someone connected to Drakkon's worst enemy. She rested her head in her hands and tried to grapple with the information.

It wasn't a surprise that she didn't belong in hell. But she never expected this. And since she was part mortal, she still wanted to figure out who her parents were, and who that woman was that she kept hearing in her dreams. She had heard the same lullaby last night when she fell asleep in the truck. Yet this Timothy remembered her, and Lynde told her that she had been the overseer of that weird place with that large winged guy.

And Marcy recollected none of it.

What she knew for sure was that she missed Mathilde and the other trainees. She would like to let them know that she was okay—Mathilde would be worried—but that couldn't happen. After the attack she had to endure with Rakye and Sorsa and all the snakes, she didn't relish the idea of getting anywhere near those beings. Even though she didn't remember this place, something about it registered inside because she felt the power and safety of the abbey.

Then she thought of Tor. Where did he fit in with all of this? Could he truly not enter into the abbey or was Lynde playing games with him?

She decided to check in on Tor as soon as she could to make sure he was okay. Until then, she went into the bathroom and ran hot water in the bathtub. Marcy perused the cabinet and found scented bath salts and shampoo. She sighed in happiness.

She sank into the water and leaned her head back, willing each muscle to relax. She fell asleep almost immediately. Marcy sensed she was in the dream. The edges of the scene were blurred. She'd seen the room before. The hospital room. The young woman singing the lullaby to the newborn. Marcy felt the evil before she turned to see the Master Demon in the room's doorway, Kraal standing beside him. Marcy watched as Kraal manipulated the humans to put down the baby, and watched as the large demon clicked his massive talons over to the infant. Watched as he lifted a talon to strike.

The dream began to quake. Marcy forced herself to stay in the dream. This was key. Something happened here, and she needed to figure it out. The room split in two as a luminous light blinded all, including Marcy. The Master Demon fought against a light-bearer, their contact shaking the foundation of the room.

The baby wailed. Marcy was just about to run and protect it when she saw Kraal pick up the baby and hide it in his cloak. Kraal stepped into the shadow and was gone.

Marcy sat up fast, splashing the now cold water out of the tub and onto the floor. "Kraal kidnapped the baby," she said to herself, getting up quickly. Her skin had turned all wrinkly, so she rubbed the towel hard against her body. She had to see Lynde. Maybe he would know what the dream meant.

If nothing else, Marcy knew she would have to seek out Kraal—

her former Shadow mentor—and find out why he had kidnapped her.

24

Two Worlds

"There she is," Timothy said, handing her a steaming plate of food. "Were you able to rest?"

"Yes, thank you. I was so tired; I fell asleep in the bathtub." She took the plate and sat down at the long bench table where Lynde already sat. He looked good. Well-rested, strong. Definitely strong. Lynde looked like the kind of guy you didn't mess with. Marcy was grateful that he was on her side. "Hi, did you take a nap?"

"I rested."

"Good."

Lynde watched her for a moment. "You look troubled."

Marcy took a bite of the roast beef and moaned in delight. "This is incredible." She dipped the thick slice of bread into the juices and devoured it. "Mortal food is simply amazing."

"It has some special seasonings," Timothy said, sitting beside Marcy. "They will make you feel good."

"Healthy," Lynde corrected. "She needs her health restored."

"Whatever the reason, the food is delicious. Thank you. I'll have to bring some to Tor."

Timothy and Lynde exchanged a brief look.

"So, why are you troubled, Marcy?" Lynde asked again.

"The same dream from before, only this time I saw that Kraal is the one that stole the baby."

"Are you sure?"

"Yes. Do you think Kraal kidnapped me?"

"You?" Timothy asked. "Why would he kidnap you?"

"Because he was my shadow mentor."

Both Lynde and Timothy stayed quiet.

"What do you two know that you're not telling? If one of you don't spill the beans, I'll step into your shadow and figure things out for myself."

"No, you won't, please." Lynde's voice went low. "That is a hellish device and tactic that we do not use. Your days as a Shadow are over."

Marcy sat back as if slapped. "What about my friends?"

"They're not your friends," Lynde said. "They are creatures of hell, Marcy. Their outcome will not turn out well. You need to forget about them."

"Forget about them?" Marcy's voice raised. "Forget about Mathilde? No, I won't. There are parts of hell that are horrible and terrifying, but Shadow trainees are only doing what they are ordered to do. They're not evil. They're...my friends!"

"Do you want to go back to hell?" Lynde asked. "Do you want to be in the cage over the inferno? Or do you want to be a slave to Drakkon? Subject to his will? Do you think it would turn out any better for those trainees?"

Timothy held up his hand to Lynde, who was getting worked

up. "Of course, you want to save your friends," Timothy said to her. "I've never experienced a Shadow. What do they do?"

"We dream weave," she explained, glad that Timothy had redirected the conversation. "We step into a mortal's shadow, and that allows us into their central circuitry unit, which is where dreams manifest from. As trainees, we are supposed to give them simple dream sequences. What we've been told by our Shadow mentors is that when we join the ranks, we will be given much more complicated tasks. We will be so skilled that we won't even have to step into a mortal's shadow. We will be able to manipulate their thoughts outside of their bodies."

"Do you understand why Drakkon would use that tactic?" Timothy asked.

"He wants to manipulate mortals to lead to some war."

"Exactly," Timothy said. "These Shadow trainees are programmed to follow orders. They operate under fear. You've probably experienced that."

"Yes," Marcy accepted, thinking about how the Guardians would disintegrate a Shadow trainee for any type of perceived rebellion. "They are afraid. That's why I want to help them."

"The greatest battle for us humans is right here." Timothy tapped his head. "The battle of our thoughts. If what you say is true, our mortal enemy, the great deceiver, manipulates our thoughts by using these agents from hell."

"They are called Shadows, and the trainees don't know that is what happens. All they know is that they swear allegiance under a

Guardian's rule and must obey orders or be disintegrated."

"You're right," Timothy said. "That doesn't sound fair. It sounds like a horrible existence." He reached for her hand. "And that is what you were? A Shadow?"

His empathy nearly brought her to tears. "Yes, I was a Shadow trainee. Until Lynde got me out." Marcy glanced at Lynde no longer feeling irritated.

The telephone rang in another room. "I have to get that. Please, excuse me." Timothy left.

Lynde got up and came and sat beside Marcy. "Forgive me for snapping at you," he said. "I can't think about losing you again. If you knew—"

"Then tell me," Marcy urged. "What do I need to know?"

Lynde trailed a finger down Marcy's face, and she wanted to melt right there. "It's complicated, and I don't want to throw too much information at you. It's a lot, especially about us. I just can't lose you again."

"You helped me in so many ways," she said to Lynde. "But these trainees don't know what they are getting into, and to think that they will be abused and tortured by Guardians or Drakkon is enough to make me turn around and try to save them."

Lynde took her hand in his. Marcy stared at their hands and felt a stirring within her. A longing. "You have always been kind and empathetic," Lynde said quietly. "Some of the many attributes I love about you."

The room became quiet. Marcy looked up and held Lynde's

gaze. "You love me?"

Timothy coughed, breaking our conversation. "It is so hard to see this. That you don't remember. How are you handling this, Michael?"

"I want to remember," I answered before Lynde—Michael—could. "What am I supposed to be remembering?"

"You already have a lot on your plate. Let's get you healthy and trained, then we'll talk again about this trainee rescue operation." Lynde stood up. "Are you ready to get started?"

"I thought I needed to rest."

"You did. You slept several hours. You just finished an excellent meal. Let's see what you can do."

"Are we going to Tor?"

"No. We've got training here that you need to prepare for first."

"Which lesson are you doing?" Timothy asked excitedly.

Lynde had already walked outside, so Timothy and Marcy followed. "She needs to remember how to fly."

Timothy cackled in delight. "I love this training."

"I'm going to fly? Like with wings?"

"Angels don't need wings." Lynde didn't stop until he stood at the edge of the cliff that overlooked the sea.

"What are you talking about, Lynde?" Marcy asked when she reached him. "I'm an angel? Like a light-bearer?"

"Yes. Hadn't you already figured it out?"

Lynde's words had a ring of truth to them. "But I'm human?"

"Partly."

"Part human. Part angel?"

"Yes."

"No Shadow?"

"No. Your angelic abilities allow you to manipulate and control many aspects of the spirit and mortal realm. Why you chose Shadow training is beyond me. Then again, you probably didn't choose. Kraal might have had something to do with it, so he could keep an eye on you. But more than that, you were probably filling divine purpose." Lynde slapped his hands together and rubbed them back and forth. "You ready?"

"Wait. You can't spring this on me now, then change the subject. How and why did I get in hell, and how and why did I become part human and part angel?"

"You know what I think?" Lynde asked, lifting Marcy by the shoulders. "I think you should stop asking questions and start figuring out how to fly."

"Why would I do that?"

"Because of this." Then Lynde twirled her around and flung her into the air with such phenomenal speed and strength that Marcy careened vertically for about ten seconds.

As gravity pulled her back down, her arms and legs flailed, and she screamed, "Lynde!!!"

Right when she thought she'd splatter on the ground, Lynde caught her in his arms. "You have to try to remember. You have the ability to maneuver in and out of spirit and mortal realms. If you remember this, it might spark all of your memories."

"Lynde," she moaned, the contents of her stomach threatening to come back up. "Don't ever do that again."

Lynde gave her a wry smile. "My name is Michael." And with that, he threw her up in the air again.

25

Time to Die

Tor ducked his head under water and scrubbed. He had already washed his clothes and left them on a rock to dry while he completely bathed himself. The river's water felt wonderful. The current wanted to take him over the ledge and down into the sea, but he managed to fight the current's strength.

Now that he was alone, and he didn't have Marcy around to make him so nervous, irritable, jealous, and every other crazy emotion that she seemed to stir up, Tor had already worked through a lot of the dilemmas. To be completely honest, he liked not being in hell. He liked that Lynde had brought them somewhere that seemed protected somehow.

Lynde.

Tor didn't know exactly who Lynde was—and the brute got under his skin—but he wasn't on Drakkon's side. The only other side was the Nameless One, so Tor wondered how that all would play out. But Tor had already told himself that he would not tell. If Drakkon did show up—and it was only a matter of time before he would—Tor would say that he was here to train Marcy, but that he had no idea where Lynde had taken her. If Drakkon asked why Tor hadn't gone back to hell and reported to him, Tor would explain that he was following strict orders to train Marcy, and her training wasn't complete. There.

Until then, he would try to put together the pieces of his memory. Like this place. Tor had been here before. The cold water woke him up and got his sluggish brain moving. The Irish Abbey seemed so familiar. When Tor got the chance, he wanted to check it out to see if it could spark something. Maybe Marcy could go with him.

The longing hit him again, taking his breath away. What was he going to do about her? Lynde warned him to stay away, and the rational part of Tor knew that he should listen. But he didn't want to listen. Every need, every desire, wrapped around her. If anything happened to her, he would be doomed from the heartbreak, so what did it matter?

He stepped out of the water and walked to the fire to dry. The sun had already set, and the stars were popping out. He slid into his pants, opting not to put the shirt on yet. He reached for his sword, but it was gone.

Tor spun around, suddenly aware of how alone—or not—he was.

His senses on alert, he waited for Drakkon to pop out of the trees or sky or something. He teleported to different places around his camp but couldn't find anything. The fighter in him was ready to pounce. Someone wanted to play games with him? Bring it.

He crouched behind a tree, determined to find the thief before the thief found him.

"Looking for this?" a voice said directly behind him. Before he could move or teleport, the butt of the sword smacked him into oblivion.

When Tor came to, his head pounded something fierce and his stomach rolled with nausea. He tried to sit up, but his head spun. Instead, he closed his eyes and let his senses tell him the situation. He lay on some sort of makeshift bed. It was hard and smooth, like a long slab of stone. A fire blazed close by, and Tor inhaled the scents of roasting meat. The scent curbed the nausea, and his stomach growled instead.

"If you can sit up, I'll give you something to eat," the voice said.

Tor turned his head toward the voice and managed to open his eyes to get a look. On the other side of the fire, a slender man stood over it, eating out of a makeshift bowl. The man couldn't have been much older than Tor. His brown hair hung in waves just past his shoulders, and his face was somewhat weathered with a few distinguished lines and the start of a beard, but there was an aura of power that came off the man in waves. It reminded him of the huge winged creature who had intimidated him earlier, not that he would ever admit that. "Who are you?"

"I should ask you the same thing since you are in my territory. You know that this sacred ground is off limits to the condemned." The man leaned over the fire and scooped what looked like stew into the bowl. "Here. Try to sit up. Let me feed you."

"Should you feed 'the condemned'?" Tor muttered with a dose of heavy sarcasm. He pushed himself up and let his feet touch the floor. Now that he got a good look around, he saw that they were inside a cave. Tor thought of Lynde setting him up on purpose, which made Tor's anger boil.

"Of course," the man said, bringing over the same bowl to Tor. "I always feed guests. Even those I have to kill." He smiled and extended the bowl.

Tor's jaw set. "I have a better idea. Why don't you go to h—"

In one swift move, the man had a short knife to Tor's neck, all while still holding the bowl. "If you know what's good for you, you will shut that mouth of yours and eat the stew that I cooked."

"I'm not hungry," Tor spat out. "So, if you're going to kill me, go ahead and do it. Stop wasting my time."

The man held Tor with supernatural strength. Tor couldn't move. But if this was his time to die, he wasn't about to go down without some sort of fight. But the man only seemed to study Tor's face with what seemed to be fascination. "How did he do it?" The man asked more to himself. A flash of grief passed over his face before he let Tor go. "Here, you need to eat. You've been in the mortal realm too long, and your humanity is growing in strength." He set the bowl in Tor's hand and put the knife away.

"What do you know about me?" Tor asked the question before he realized how vulnerable it sounded. But if this man had any idea, Tor didn't want to lose the opportunity.

"I know that you're hungry, and you need to eat. There is a

battle coming, and you will need all your strength for it." The man walked back over to the fire. He paused before speaking again as if weighing his words. "You have been marked as a servant of Drakkon. Your anger, hostility, and aversion to your own truth only verify the mark. You've been around evil too long. You don't know how to behave, or what to do when others are trying to help. You've been brutally abused so that you can be a submissive soldier with unwavering loyalty." When he looked up at Tor, the man appeared grim. "Does that sum it up?"

Tor's annoyance increased. He was more annoyed with himself for even asking the question. "Who are you? Since you already seem to know me."

"Call me Eli."

"What do you do out here in the cave?"

"I inhabit the entire forest. I'm a prophet of the Most High, also known as the Lord of Hosts."

"The Nameless One?"

Eli chuckled and shook his head. "Ah, that's right. In hell, His name is not spoken."

Tor ignored the condescending behavior. "A prophet? So, you're psychic?" Drakkon used fortunetellers often to prophesy the future.

"The gifts I've been given are for good. For people's eyes to be opened to truth. Truth, above all else, must be protected."

Tor hadn't realized he had eaten the entire contents of the bowl until he was scraping the bottom.

"Have you noticed your appetite's increased?" Eli asked, taking the bowl and filling it again.

"Yes, and my thirst."

"The longer you stay in the mortal realm, the more time your humanity—what little bit was left—has a chance to flourish and grow. That's why Drakkon didn't expose you to this world very often."

"And the nausea?"

"Your spirit is rejecting the elements of hell." Eli handed him a canteen of water. "You've been enslaved, Tor. Now that you're here, who you are inside is rejecting what you've been forced to accept. That makes you dangerous. Very dangerous. When Drakkon finds you now, he won't take any chances."

"He'll kill me?"

"Probably far worse."

"How do you know all of this?"

"That's why I knocked you out. So, I could read you. Without interruption."

"Well, I'm fed," Tor said. "I guess that means you have to kill me now. It's probably best. I'd rather you do it than Drakkon. Just do me a favor and tell Lynde that I will haunt him from hell and make his existence miserable for sabotaging me like this."

"Technically," Eli clarified. "I'm supposed to kill any creature of the condemned. But you are also human, which makes this a bit more complicated." Eli picked up Tor's sword. He maneuvered it effortlessly. "So, I guess the decision is up to you. Where are your loyalties?"

Tor knew a baited question when asked. "I'm loyal to myself."

"Lie!" Eli said. He disappeared right in front of Tor. Tor felt the sword cut across his forearm. Since the sword was laced with the poison of hell, he groaned in agony, falling to the ground. "Where are your loyalties?"

Tor searched to find Eli, but he evidently had the power to be invisible.

Eli asked the question again, but Tor couldn't catch his breath as the poison made its way through his system. "Just kill me!" Tor shouted. "What does it matter where my loyalties lie?"

Eli materialized in front of him. "Because it matters, Tor."

Tor took the chance and lunged at the man, wrestling with him for the sword. Tor threw punches, but Eli was fast. Tor tried to teleport, but his injury was too overpowering. But he wouldn't die without swinging. He threw fireballs at Eli, as the prophet dodged each one.

Suddenly Eli was behind him, riding his back. Tor slammed him against the wall, despite the knife being at his neck. "Where do your loyalties lie, Tor?"

"*I don't know*!" Tor shouted before flipping Eli off of him.

Eli rounded with a swift kick across Tor's face, knocking him to the ground. Tor pushed himself up, panting. "That's the wrong answer," Eli said, as he walked closer, the sword pointed at Tor.

"Go ahead," Tor said. "I want to die."

Eli stood over him, a small smile playing on his lips. "Now *that*,

Tor, is the right answer." He lifted the sword before pushing it through Tor's chest.

26

True Guardian

Marcy lay on the bed and stared at the ceiling. Trying to fly was a complete failure, and her muscles hurt. Not to mention her pride.

There was a knock at the door, but Marcy could only turn her head and say, "If it's Timothy, come in. If it's Lynde, go away."

The door opened, and Timothy walked in with a tray. "I brought some things that will help you feel better."

"Then please come in."

He set the tray down and helped her sit up. Her muscles groaned in response. "Take this, and drink this." Timothy gave her a couple of pills and a warm mug of tea.

"Thank you."

He dragged a chair over and sat down. "It's bizarre," he said, as she sipped the tea. "That you have no memory."

Marcy nodded. It bothered her, too. If she was who they thought she was, she would like to remember. "Can you explain it to me? I'm trying to piece it together, but Lynde is being cryptic."

"Michael is a warrior at heart, but trust me when I say that he loves you very much. You two have quite the history. I think he's trying to protect you, and maybe his own heart."

Marcy stopped drinking and swallowed. "What kind of

history?"

"You were—are—angelic betrothed. The power couple of heaven. Both fierce warriors, whose passion for each other came only under your passionate devotion to God."

Marcy nearly dropped the mug. "Me and Lynde? Together?" Butterflies released internally. She might not have remembered, but the thought of the two of them together made her feel a mix of nerves and excitement. She had tried to ignore whatever attraction she had felt because there had been too much going on to really give it attention.

"It's Michael, and yes, together."

She closed her eyes and tried to envision the two of them. Now that Lynde was Michael, and he had shed the grotesque features he had used for a façade in hell, he was powerfully attractive. He was powerful, period. Then she remembered his fierce protection when Rakye attacked her. She remembered how he saved her from the cage. Shoot, he had been the one to save her from hell. She pressed a hand to her heart. "How had I not seen that?"

"That's what we're trying to piece together. When you decided to be born as a human, something happened. My best guess is that your humanity is blocking your memory. Do you have—feel— anything toward Michael?"

As soon as he asked the question, she thought of the connection she had felt with Lynde since traveling together. The way she felt warmth when he touched her hand or smiled her way. "All of this is new to me," she said. "Plus, he's not on my nice list after the flying fiasco."

Timothy smiled. "Yes, I understand. Michael is so desperate for you to remember that I'm afraid that trumped tenderness. There is a way…well, never mind. That's between you and Michael."

"There's a way to what?"

"It's not my place, but ask Michael. He'll tell you what you can do to remember." Timothy stood up. "He wants to come and check on you. Will you see him, or do you want me to tell him to go away?"

Marcy was so dumbfounded at what Timothy had just revealed to her, that she didn't know what to think or say. She finally nodded when she saw he still waited for an answer.

When Timothy left, Marcy's head whirled at the news. It blew her mind, yet at the same time, the energy within her recognized the truth of Timothy's words. A part of her was desperate to believe it. She had ignored the feelings of desire out of confusion and exhaustion. And there was also Tor. She didn't feel the same way toward him, yet there was a wildness and unpredictability about him that was exhilarating. What would he do when he found out about Marcy's past life?

She shook her head. She couldn't think about Tor right now. Bigger issues hung around her neck. For starters, if she truly was a light-bearer, why had she and Lynde—Michael—gone to hell? Was it some kind of special mission? Had they completed what they were supposed to do?

There was a soft knock before Lynde poked his head in. "May I enter?"

He looked apologetic, but Marcy still glowered at him. "I guess." She pushed herself the rest of the way up and let her feet come to the floor.

After he shut the door, he came and sat in the same chair that Timothy had sat in. He scooted it over to sit directly in front of Marcy. "I'm sorry. I hoped and anticipated that you'd remember the skill."

"Whoever I was before I was Marcy, I might not ever be her again. Is that what you're afraid of?"

The pained expression on his face hit Marcy's heart. He did love her. How had she missed it? She reached out and took his hand. It was enormous compared to hers. He covered her hand with his other one. "Deborah," he said quietly. "Your name is Deborah. At least it was. Kraal named you Marcy."

"Did you disguise yourself and endure hell to get me out?"

"Yes."

"Why was I there in the first place? And how come you are not part human like I am?"

Lynde rubbed his face before holding her hand again. "You volunteered to guard the human baby who was to be born the anomaly in mankind's final century. At least before Drakkon waged war. It was prophesied that this baby would tip the scales of victory for Drakkon. The protection of the baby's soul was of utmost importance."

Marcy's head exploded at the memory. "The baby in the

hospital," she gasped. "That wasn't me?"

Lynde shook his head. "No, when you got there, Kraal and Zorel were already there. You fought gloriously."

The truth sucker-punched her. "Kraal kidnapped the baby while I was fighting."

"Yes."

Marcy stood up and pushed past Lynde. "I failed."

"That's what sent you into a panic. If you had talked to me, we would have figured something out, but the next thing I know, you've already attacked Kraal and made a deal."

Marcy spun around; her eyes wide in shock. "Kraal has been involved since the beginning?"

"Yes. He had already given the baby to Drakkon. You had to go to hell to retrieve him. To access hell, you decided to be reborn. By then, I couldn't stop you. You were gone. And Kraal tricked you. Put you in the lowest ranking class, so that you would never cross paths with Drakkon or…Tor."

"Tor," she whispered his name, as the truth rested squarely on her shoulders. "My job was to protect him." Marcy looked guiltily at Lynde. "If Kraal meant to keep me separated, how did I get to be involved with Tor and Drakkon?"

"Divine destiny. It's beautiful. It's where everything comes together, even when everything in hell works to keep it from happening."

"I had to save the baby though. My plan turned out wrong, too. Because I didn't remember. I still don't remember! So now I'm stuck not remembering, and Tor is still in danger."

Lynde grunted. "Yes, he's in some serious danger."

"It's still my duty to protect him, isn't it?"

Lynde looked so pained that Marcy felt for him, but now that the truth was revealed, the energy hummed in a mix of relief and expectancy. Marcy had a job to do. "The unexpected complication was that being born into hell completely severed your memory. You are still all angel, but there's this human part of you that is hindering you from remembering."

Marcy sat down again next to him. "I need to remember, Lynde. Please. Timothy said you know of a way. What's keeping you from doing it?"

"Because it's been prophesied that I have to give you the choice. Trust me, if it was up to me, I would have done it when I first found you in Levea."

"What is it? Whatever it is, I choose for you to do it."

"You have to know the ramifications." Lynde's eyes found hers. "You and I have a history."

"I know," Marcy said carefully. "Timothy told me. I'm sorry that I don't remember."

Lynde took a deep breath. "Because we are betrothed in heaven, all we would have to do would be to become one."

Marcy nodded. "One? As in…"

Lynde wouldn't look Marcy in the eye. "Yes. Our union would be honored. All my memories would be shared with you. We would truly be one in heart, mind, and body."

Her heart banged in her chest. The butterflies had yet to settle down. But there was one hindering thought. "What about Tor?"

"I know you care for him. That is why I haven't said anything."

"I do care for him, but not necessarily in the way you think. I feel drawn to him, and I never understood why. But it's because I'm sworn to protect him. It is strong within me. He needs my help."

"If you kiss me, Deborah," Lynde said. "It may spark something. I'm not saying that to trick you. It's not in me to be dishonest. It was Timothy's idea. Not that I haven't thought about it. Trust me when I say that there's nothing I want more. For twenty mortal years, I've lived without you, and even though that's not even a drop in the bucket when it comes to eternity, it was agony nonetheless."

Marcy studied Lynde as if seeing him for the first time. How he must have suffered when she chose to go to hell to save the baby without even telling him first. How hard it must have been for twenty years for him to endure hell just to find her. The tears leaked from her eyes, as her heart filled with gratitude. "I would have had to endure an eternity of servitude," she whispered. "They would have broken me."

"I would never let that happen."

"You were stuck in hell for all those years, and I can't even remember—" She wiped futilely at the tears.

Lynde stood up and with some hesitation stepped over to her. He cupped his hand on her face. "This is why I didn't tell you. I don't want you to feel guilty."

"But I do."

"You did what needed to be done."

"But if I had talked to you first."

"One thing I've learned being an angel is never to question destiny. What happened was supposed to have happened. And if it's meant to be, we will be together again." Lynde—Michael—trailed his hand down her face. She leaned into him. "We have all of eternity. I don't mind waiting a little longer."

"I don't understand my feelings or emotions. I'm exhilarated at the prospect of us, but I also feel guilty because of Tor."

"You went there to save him. You have a connection with him that will never go away. And that is why I haven't kissed you." Lynde took a step back. "And why I'm not going to, not unless you ask. No matter how difficult, I will give you the space you need to figure things out." He walked to the door. "Just be careful. I was serious when I told you earlier that Tor is not only in danger, but he is extremely dangerous. I don't know what I would do if…well, it's not good to dwell on what ifs."

The words were there to call Lynde back to her. To ask him to kiss her. Every part of her desired him. It could be the chance she needed to remember. To find these lost feelings for Lynde…no, *Michael*. Instead, she said, "I have a lot to think about. And I'll have to tell Tor. He deserves to know."

Lynde nodded. "I know. See you in the morning? We'll head over there for training. We don't look the same, so he'll be demanding some answers."

The two of them shared a smile.

"For what it's worth, I desire when this is all said and done, for us to start again."

"I'd like that." He shut the door behind him, which left Marcy staring after him.

She felt a twinge of regret. She had this longing for Lynde that scared her. It was intense and hungry. Yet, every time her thoughts went to Lynde, thoughts of Tor weren't far behind. That's why she hadn't kissed Lynde right then and there. She was too worried about Tor. She was sworn to protect him, and now that she knew the truth of her past, she refused for anything to get in the way of that promise.

Taking a deep breath, Marcy decided to stop wasting time. She needed to talk to Tor. It would be an uncomfortable conversation, but it needed to be done.

27

Reborn

Someone was calling his name. A woman's voice. Sweet, gentle. He turned toward her, but he couldn't see anything past the blinding light. "Who is it?" he called.

His name again. He moved toward her voice. Her tone increased in desperation. Was she crying? Tor started to run, but he couldn't see anything other than a vast whiteness that burned his vision.

"Tor? Tor?"

He heard Marcy's voice this time, and it stopped him. Marcy? The bright light was gone, as he began to come to. It was then he felt the hard, cold ground he was laying upon. He remembered what happened, the way the sword felt going through his chest. Shouldn't he be dead? Maybe he was. Maybe Drakkon was playing tricks on him.

"Tor?"

He felt her touch on his bare shoulder, felt the closeness of her breath as she inspected him. He decided to pretend to be out of it for a moment more. Until he felt her hand over his heart. His breath caught, and his eyes opened. It was beating.

"Hey," she whispered.

"Hey." Tor swallowed; his throat dry. He felt his arms, chest, and legs. He seemed to be in one piece. He pushed himself up on his elbows, wincing from where the sword had cut him. So, it *had* happened.

"Why are you outside in the middle of the night alone? Couldn't you find the cave?"

"Because you deserted me."

"You act like you're in pain."

"I need water," he said, slightly out of breath.

"I came prepared." Marcy slid off the straps of a duffle bag that hung around her shoulders. She opened it up. "I have some soap, some food, a toothbrush, and…" She held up a water bottle.

"Do you mind?" Tor indicated that he needed the water. He felt vulnerable being so weak, but his strength had seemed to vanish.

She opened up the bottle and brought it to his lips.

Tor took it and guzzled. When he finished, he handed it back to her and laid back down. "Are you here alone? Where's Lynde?"

He watched her look away. The guilt and struggle on her face were so easy to read. Even though the outside fire still blazed—that Eli guy must have been keeping it going—he didn't like not seeing her face. He reached up and gently turned her to him.

Something about her countenance stole his breath away. Her blue eyes shone like beacons in the darkness, and her skin with her high cheekbones and slight nose was flawless. The aura around her was similar to what he felt around Eli. "You're a light-bearer," he whispered, the truth finally descending upon him. She was an angel of light, and he was a master of darkness.

His heart crashed to the ground at the thought. Tor would never be able to deserve her. He smiled sadly and went to move his hand away. He could now see with clarity. Their paths were too far separated for any of Tor's fantasies of the future to be fulfilled.

"We have to talk," she whispered. "I don't want to hurt you. I've already failed on so many levels." She had tears in her eyes.

Tor sat up again and noticed the scar on his chest, but he would deal with that later. All that mattered now was Marcy.

He wrapped his one arm around her and pulled her to him.

Marcy placed her hands on his chest. "Tor," she turned her head. "We have to talk. This can't happen. That's what I came to tell you."

A loud boom exploded in his ears, and he was suddenly airborne. He fell into the cold water, sinking deep. He swam up, aware of how kludgy he felt. When he broke the surface, he took in a breath and prepared to meet an onslaught of demons or something sinister. Instead, he saw Eli standing over Marcy as if protecting her.

Anger had always been his fallback emotion. But he was more frustrated than angry. The cold water did little to calm the raging desire still burning inside of him. "You could have just interrupted us. No need to throw me in the water," Tor grumbled as he trudged over to Eli.

"Do you know who that is?" Eli hissed at Tor. "You don't defile an angel of light. Ever. Not without serious consequences."

Tor combed his hair with his fingers and turned away from Eli.

He acted nonchalantly, but he heard the truth of the prophet's words. Once again, he should have been angry. But he wasn't. This time, he felt guilty. Guilty because if Eli hadn't stopped him, he would have easily given in to temptation.

"Are you okay?" Marcy asked Tor, approaching him. She touched his arm, tentatively, acting unsure how he would react.

Had he been that bad of a loose cannon?

"Yeah, I'm fine. How are you?"

"I don't know. I have a million thoughts going through my head." She looked directly at Eli, who was watching her in apparent disbelief. "Who is that?"

Eli didn't answer. Instead, he asked, "Who are you, and what did you do with Deborah?"

"I'm Marcy," she said. "I have no recollection of Deborah."

"Obviously," he said. "Poor Michael. Does he know about the two of you?" Eli indicated Marcy and Tor.

"Who's Michael?" Tor asked, trying to piece together what they were talking about. It didn't slip past Tor's attention that Marcy had some sort of knowledge already.

"Michael is Deborah's betrothed."

"Stop it," Marcy demanded Eli.

"He needs to know," Eli said. "There is no deception in this place. There are no lies or trickery. Do not keep it from him."

"Keep what from me?"

"I'm going to tell him in my own time. I just wanted to say goodbye."

"Why are you talking like I'm not here?" Tor asked Marcy. He grabbed her arm and turned her to him. Wow, did she look different. Radiant. Mesmerizing. And a thousand other words, but it still wouldn't do her justice. "Who's Michael?"

Marcy's face crumpled. "I only wanted to tell you in my own way," she said and shot a glare at Eli.

"Who's Michael?" he asked again.

Sighing, she said, "Lynde."

Tor watched her face, putting Eli's words with what she just said. "Lynde is Michael?" he said more to himself. "And you are… Deborah?"

Marcy covered her face. "I don't remember it. I'm trying, but I can't remember."

Tor took a step back. "If Lynde is Michael, and you are Deborah, then the two of you are—what's the word—betrothed?"

"Yes," Eli said, jumping in for Marcy, who was too busy crying. "They are betrothed."

"So, Marcy's a defender of the Nameless One?"

"He has a name, but yes."

The ache inside of Tor increased with every breath he took. He pressed against his chest. "This doesn't make sense," he said, trying to breathe. "Why would you two be in hell? Were you spies?"

Marcy wiped her eyes and looked at Tor. "All of this is new to me. As in I was informed not even a day ago. What I know is that I was raised a Shadow trainee. That's it. Now, there's another side of the story. One that involves kidnapping and betrayal. And failure. Definitely failure."

"You do not remember anything?" Eli asked Marcy.

"Nothing. I dream of the hospital room. In the dream, Kraal takes the baby. That's it. I'm assuming it's a memory, but I can't recall anything else."

"What's there to remember?" Tor asked, trying to wrap his head around the news. "And what does Kraal have to do with taking a baby?"

"I was in charge of protecting a human baby anomaly. One that would help fight with humanity in the war brought on by Drakkon. The baby's location was discovered by hell, and when I found out and arrived, I fought and destroyed the demon set on killing the child."

Tor had an uneasy feeling about where this was going.

"While the fight was happening, a Shadow stole the baby right out from under my nose and fled. When I caught up to him, it was too late. The baby had been handed over to Drakkon."

The news shouldn't have surprised him. He had to have been kidnapped. Tor had already figured that out. But Marcy had been there? It seemed ludicrous. "You want me to believe that you were my guardian, and you failed your task, and I was kidnapped anyway?"

"I'm so sorry," she whispered.

Tor closed his eyes and relived some of the worst torture sessions he endured. "I have never had a normal life."

"I know," Marcy whispered again, almost as if the words were too much.

"I've been beaten, abused, assaulted, tortured…" Tor stopped as the emotions—the very emotions he had bottled up for over twenty mortal years—came out like a torrent. His vision became blurry, and he wiped at his eyes. Tears?

"Deborah did the only thing she could," Eli said quietly. "She was reborn part mortal to hide her light-bearer status. She was determined to find you and bring you to safety. Unfortunately, the birthing process has given her amnesia or—what I'm really afraid of—it eliminated her memories."

Tor tried to process the information, but the only two details that stuck out were that Marcy and Lynde were a couple and that Tor was nothing more than a project gone bad.

"There is good news," Eli said to both of them. Tor glanced over at him and waited. When Eli had Marcy's attention, too, he continued, "You have been rescued. You are here, and you are safe. Deborah and Michael have been successful. No harm can come to you while under my protection."

"Your protection?" Tor asked with a humorless laugh. "You put a sword through my heart!"

"He did?" Marcy asked Tor.

Eli shook his head at the both of them. "Of course, I did. I had to kill the root of evil that had attached to your spirit. You are not the same. You feel it, no?"

"I feel weak, and my chest hurts. Two very good reasons not to want you as my protection."

Eli grinned at Tor, nodding in enthusiasm. "Good, good. You are weak because you have been stripped of your powers, and your chest hurts because—"

"Whoa! Go back a second. What did you say?"

"You've been stripped of your powers."

Tor stepped back as if he'd been slapped. He lifted his hand and tried to summon fire. Nothing. He struggled to breathe. Tor leaned over, resting his hands on his knees. "What did you do? Why would you do that?"

"You said you wanted to die. That was your spirit talking through you, Tor." Eli took a step closer to him. "Now you are a human again with a clean slate inside. That way we can train you in the ways of light and truth. This is what was meant to be."

"Really?" Marcy asked with hope in her voice.

"Your powers will slowly come back to you, but without the evil attached," Eli said to Tor.

"Will I still have power over fire? And travel between realms? And control the mortal's atmosphere?"

"Technically, you have power over all the elements. Fire, wind, water, and earth. It is subject to you because you will need that gift in the upcoming battle. The same goes for everything else. But these gifts need to regrow in a more positive direction."

"So, I was kidnapped by hell, tortured and abused for years, and now I'm stripped of my powers." Tor looked from Eli to Marcy. "Well, I guess that means you won. Congratulations. If you excuse me, I'd like to be alone."

"Tor, please forgive me," Marcy called after him. "But you're here, and you're safe."

"From what?" Tor spun around to glare at her. "In hell, I was powerful. I was Drakkon's right-hand man. What made you think that I would want this? Did you ask?"

Marcy moved toward him.

"Don't. I want to be alone. You've done enough already."

Tor stumbled through the dark woods. Without the aid of fire or the ability to travel with powers, he felt kludgy and weak. He paused when the trees opened up to the ocean. The drop to the crashing waves couldn't be far, so he fell onto the ground and tried to regain normal breathing. He wiped at the sweat that dripped from his forehead, and he felt the immediate thirst. He didn't think to grab water.

"Here." Eli sat beside him and handed him a canister of water.

"I want to be alone."

"I know. I also knew you'd be thirsty." Eli got up to leave.

"I can't go back, can I?"

"The real question is whether or not you really want to."

"I don't want to be this." Tor lifted his hands, only to drop them. He took a swig of the cold liquid and wiped his mouth. "I'm weak. I've never been weak a day in my life."

"Sure, you were. You were called weak when you cried genuine tears in hell over the mortal souls falling into the lake of fire. That was one of the first times Drakkon flung you into outer darkness."

A chill shot up Tor's spine. "How do you know that?"

Eli didn't answer. "Drakkon beat or tortured the weakness out of you, but was it weakness? No, it was compassion, empathy, and a sense of justice. Things that cannot exist in hell."

"They do not exist in the mortal realm either. Mortals are selfish and hedonistic and angry. They are a miserable lot, and they deserve what they get."

"Some are, but not all. And is that Tor talking, or is that what you were trained to say?" Eli paused, then continued, "What happened to the family you came across during the last hurricane you produced."

Tor stopped drinking water and stared at Eli. "No one knows about that. How do you know?"

"What happened to the family, Tor? The tsunami came, and you saw the little boy holding a light pole, screaming for his mother."

"Stop."

"What happened when the mother came running to him, mere seconds before the wave hit?"

Tor closed his eyes and remembered the scene. It was too late to stop the water from crashing upon them. He moved without thinking. He teleported to them, grabbed them both, and teleported them to a rooftop. Had it only been months ago? "I didn't want the child dying. So what?"

"Was that the only time?"

"Why are you doing this?"

"Because, Tor, you don't belong in hell. Most humans don't. Hell wasn't created for you or them. And you know it. It was something Drakkon couldn't beat out of you, no matter how hard he tried. Is that what you want to go back to?" Eli added, "You may feel weak right now, but trust me, Tor, you are exactly where you need to be. Trust the process."

"But if I'm weak, how can I defend myself?"

"Drakkon cannot enter these sacred grounds. Only those with a willingness toward goodness and truth can."

"How did Lynde know that I could enter here? I've been in hell. There is no goodness or truth in me."

"Because Michael didn't just go to hell to retrieve Deborah. He was there for you too. He trusted that there was some small source of goodness in you. Enough to let you walk in and be freed."

"So, I don't have to go back?" Tor asked. "As long as I stay here on these sacred grounds, I'll be safe?"

"You are free, Tor. Absolutely and completely free."

"And my powers?"

"I'm not sure how they will manifest once you heal and we begin training. They will still control the elements, but I'm not sure to what extent. Being an ally to the light will come with multiple gifts, as well as multiple responsibilities."

Tor lifted his head to the night sky and stared at the stars, letting Eli's words sink inside. If what he said was true, Tor was free. Free from torment. Free from Drakkon and his evil ways. It was a new feeling running through his veins. There was freedom outside of hell that he never experienced before. He never allowed himself to hope before this moment. "Are you sure there is no possible way for Drakkon or any of his minions to get in here? I'm just verifying."

Eli knelt beside Tor and rested his hand on his shoulder. "Unless he gets a direct invitation from the Most High Himself, Drakkon or anything else from hell without a seed of goodness cannot step foot on this sacred land."

"I can be free?" Tor whispered up at the sky.

"You are already free," Eli answered. "The only way to go back is if you choose to."

"No," Tor said, then looked back at Eli, letting a full smile transform his face. When was the last time he smiled? A real smile? "I'm not going back. But I do need to regain my strength. When do we start training."

"Easy there. Your body needs to heal, but you're already doing better than I expected."

"Which means?"

"Which means sooner rather than later."

Tor pushed himself up off the ground. "I need to find Marcy. She needs to stop feeling guilty."

"Being alone with her is not good. Your love for her is easy to read. You've got to let it go."

"Love?" Tor asked. "I've never known love."

"Yes, you have. Because she loves you, but maybe not in the way you would want."

Eli was right. "I love her," he whispered. The words felt foreign on his tongue, but they felt right. "I would do anything for her. I can't see her distraught like this. Let me go and talk to her."

"And then what?"

"She feels guilty, and I didn't help with making her feel any better, did I? But without her, I wouldn't be here with a chance to start over. I want her to know that I choose this."

"Fine, but only for a few minutes. She refuses to use the shadows for travel, which means she is still on foot. That direction." Eli pointed in the direction of the abbey and then disappeared immediately.

Tor ran partly, but walked mostly, calling after Marcy. It felt weird, the whole human thing. He was slower, and he could feel the lack of his former power. Yet, now that he was no longer upset, he could feel some kind of warm energy, spreading from where the sword went through. It tingled and burned at the same time.

Sweat poured off of him as he plowed through the forest, finally finding the path that led to the abbey. He eventually found her, nearly to the edge of the sacred forest. "Marcy!"

Marcy stopped and turned.

Tor had to catch his breath. Luckily, she waited for him and headed toward him, closing the gap.

"This is really weird. I've never been winded before."

"Eli seems to know what he's doing," she said. "He thinks you will feel better and stronger soon."

"I already feel better."

"Really?" She looked unconvinced. "You were upset, not that I blame you."

"It was a lot to throw at a guy, okay?"

"Yeah, I guess it was."

"But the more I think about it, the more I realize what you and Lynde did for me was pretty incredible. I mean, I don't have to spend eternity serving Drakkon. I never thought that was possible." Tor glanced around, knowing Eli was somewhere close. Tor felt the words bubble up inside of him. "I love you."

Marcy opened her mouth in surprise. Her face crumpled, and tears came. "Please, don't tell me that. My heart isn't yours to love. I can't…we can't…"

The truth began to illuminate his heart as he sorted through his feelings. "I loved you from the moment you sent me careening down the waterfall. You were the light I needed to see how much I hated that place." Tor needed to continue. He didn't want to, but it was the truth, and it needed to be said. "And you kept enduring my evilness over and over. I don't deserve you. Any man who tries to kill a woman isn't a man at all. He's a monster."

"You were only doing what you were trained to do."

"When you screamed, it wasn't me who saved you. I was too afraid. I didn't want Drakkon to find out my feelings for you. Instead, Lynde saved you. He didn't care what Drakkon thought. All I could do was watch you hanging over the inferno, but I didn't have the guts to save you. Lynde was there for you over and over again."

The tears were gone, as Marcy studied him with a thoughtful expression. "He did do that, but Tor, I don't blame you."

"Of course, you don't. You are, after all, a light-bearer. But I don't deserve you. I know it, and I think you know it too. You went to hell to save me, and you did. I'll be okay. I know it." His throat constricted. "And you're not even Marcy anymore. Look at yourself. You're Deborah."

He leaned down and kissed her cheek. It was wet with her tears. Even though it killed him, he turned and left her standing in the woods. He understood what Lynde meant when he warned Tor to leave her alone. Tor thought that Lynde was merely a jealous Guardian, maybe a bit threatened. But no. Whether he wanted to admit it or not, Lynde always had Marcy's best intentions at the forefront of everything he did. And he helped Tor escape from hell. Tor fought him every step of the way, but he was starting to see the real Lynde. And it made Tor pale in comparison. He stopped and turned, second-guessing himself, but she had already left. Tor closed his eyes and whispered, "Goodbye."

28

Distractions

Marcy stayed on the path that detoured to a lookout point at the cliff.

Tor's words replayed over in her mind. He loved her, but he wasn't good enough for her. She understood that what he said was true. He did try to kill her, but he was under Drakkon's influence. She easily forgave him, but why didn't she say the words to him? She did love him, but she kept the words to herself. Was it because she didn't want to give him false hope? Her thoughts turned to Michael, and she understood why she did not say the words in return. Michael truly held her heart. She didn't need to remember everything from her past to understanding the longing she felt when with him.

She found a lone bench that overlooked the Irish Sea and sat down. It was a steep drop, but Marcy wasn't paying any attention. Her eyes were focused on the first sunrise she had ever observed. The sun's rays streaked across the sky as it climbed out from the sea.

Despite the confusion that plagued her, she watched it and marveled.

"It's beautiful, isn't it?"

She turned to the voice beside her, unsurprised to see him. Then again, there was a calmness to this sanctuary that had no fear. Something else she marveled. "I would like to be alone."

"I never was able to sneak up on you," Eli said, ignoring her statement. "Before you left us, it was a game we'd play. But you always seemed to know I was there."

"I wish I could remember."

Eli paused before saying, "Are you angry? Tor was angry too, but I calmed him down. Talk to me. I can help."

"I'm frustrated. There's a difference. I desperately want to remember my past while at the same time I feel guilty for the years of torture and abuse Tor endured. So many feelings. Not sure what to do with any of them."

"The end is coming, Deborah," he said. "I know you don't realize how big a role you play, but you play a pretty big role."

"I helped Tor get here, so I would think my assignment has been accomplished."

"That was only part of the assignment. You were to guard the human anomaly, and when he became of age, you and Michael were to train him to be a warrior for the Most High."

"You know what I don't quite understand? How did Kraal and that demon get to the baby before me? How did they know?"

"Drakkon is aware of the prophecies, Deborah. That's why he is such a dangerous threat. But you're right. That doesn't explain how they slipped in. I've thought about that these last twenty years, and the only answer that feels right is we were betrayed."

Marcy stopped looking at the sunrise long enough to study Eli. His face had strong features, handsome in a timeless way, much like Michael's, but there was a wisdom that also lined his features, an understanding that demonstrated he knew what he was talking about. She knew that he meant what he said when he stated that there were no lies or deception in this place. Even Tor, who was raised in hell, had been honest. Brutally so, but honest all the same. "Betrayed?" she finally asked. The energy inside of her hummed in agreement. So, it felt it too?

"Yes. It can't be one of us. It has to be one of the humans we work with. They are the fallible ones that Drakkon can get to and manipulate. But nothing out of the ordinary has happened these last twenty years. I've scanned the few humans we work with, and none of them display anything that would demonstrate their lack of loyalty."

"What does that mean?"

"It means that they might not even know they've been disloyal."

Marcy closed her eyes and breathed deeply. The salt air was intoxicating. She couldn't imagine being disloyal to these light-bearers. "Where do I come in?"

"You are in a dangerous predicament. By being part human, you have the same highs and lows of emotion, which means that Drakkon can manipulate you. That's why Tor is still dangerous, too, especially now that his powers have been stripped. If Drakkon gets his hands on either one of you, then we are right back where we started."

"But you need Tor to fight the war, right?"

"To protect humanity. The second part of the prophecy involves you. You and Michael."

"Great. I can't even figure out who I am, and now I've got to add a prophecy to it."

Eli smiled sadly. "I know you still see yourself as this Marcy, but trust me when I say that Deborah is in there." He pointed to Marcy's heart. "Channel her, and you will shed this Marcy persona forever."

"What happens if I don't want to?" Marcy shook her head, suddenly fed up with prophecies and rumors of wars. "What happens if Marcy is now who I am? What happens then?"

"*It can't be!*" he said, his words trembling the ground. "That is your humanity talking! Only selfishness would say 'I want to hold on to the familiar.' That's a human trait. This involves sacrifice and selflessness."

"I don't even know what I'm fighting for!"

"You and Michael lead the charge into hell. You tear down the dark kingdom for eternity. Drakkon doesn't stand a chance against Deborah. But he does against Marcy. He knows that. He's desperate. You will have to fight him and defeat him. And you cannot do that as a partial human!" He stood up, a wave of righteous anger coming from him. Marcy's energy thrummed in the same rhythm as if it was angry too. "Channel the Deborah inside of you before Drakkon figures out what's going on." Suddenly Eli's eyes widened. "No," he whispered.

"What?" Marcy then felt the energy shift. "Tor!"

"Get Michael now!" Eli vanished from her sight.

Marcy started running toward the abbey, but it was so far away. "Michael!!!!" she yelled. "Michael!!"

He landed on his feet right in front of her. "Where is he?"

"I left him in the woods."

"I need you to go to the abbey and inform Timothy what's going on. He needs to message the angelic army. Go!"

"But what about Tor?"

"Trust me, I will protect him."

Marcy started to run.

"Deborah!" he called.

She turned. "Yes?"

"Please, stay there. It's safe, and I can't lose you again."

Marcy nodded and began to run again.

"Fly!" Michael yelled at her as he headed in the opposite direction.

Fly? Marcy couldn't fly! Still, she tried to summon her energy to do it. Instead, she got winded from running. She was tempted to travel by shadow, but she wanted nothing to do with hellish devices anymore.

When she finally reached the abbey, Timothy came running out, his eyes bloodshot and his red hair wild.

"What's happening out there? You were gone, and then Michael took off. I'm worried."

"Is there anyone who would betray this place? Even if they

didn't know they were doing it?"

"No, not that I know. Only Levi is allowed to enter, and he is devout. Michael has never sensed betrayal or deception from him. But what if…" Timothy's face crumpled. "Levi does something on accident?"

"Like what?"

"Levi has worked with me for over twenty years. When he asked to take food to the stranded warrior, I believed him to be helping, but now it might have been a trick. Levi might be a pawn, and he doesn't even know it."

"Levi? The man from yesterday?"

"Yes. He has never let me down."

"And he asked to take food to Tor?"

"Just this morning. He wanted to help. Michael might have been able to read any deceit or trickery, but he was too distracted because you… Oh, that doesn't matter."

"Because I left," Marcy said quietly. "I left to pursue Tor, which distracted Michael, which allowed this Levi to get to Tor."

Timothy shook his head. "Oh no, no, no. Don't blame yourself. And don't blame Levi. I…I…I don't know what I will do if you leave us again." He broke down in tears.

"We're both human," Marcy said, placing her hand on Timothy's shoulder. "Which means we make mistakes."

He nodded, even though his hands covered his face to muffle the sobs.

Marcy looked toward the woods and wondered what was

happening. She fought with the idea of staying put, but for once, she needed to listen to Michael.

But Tor...

He was her responsibility. And this whole mess landed squarely on her shoulders. If she hadn't been so driven to see Tor one last time, Michael would have easily discerned that Levi was at the very least being manipulated by darker forces. And she had distracted Eli, too. If he hadn't talked to her at the cliff, he would have stopped the security breach.

Once again, it was Marcy's fault.

Suddenly, Michael appeared beside them. His face was grim. Marcy knew the answer before he said the words.

"Tor's gone. He's left our boundaries."

And with those words, the guilt, once again, fell heavily on Marcy's shoulders.

29

Deception

As soon as he reached the clearing by the ruins, the tingling and burning of his scar burst inside of him, spreading throughout his body. He fell to his knees, his body trembling from the sheer force of the energy.

That's when he heard someone calling his name. It wasn't Marcy. The voice was distinctly male. "Tor?" the voice got closer. "Is there a Tor back here?"

Tor wanted to move quickly but couldn't. The energy burst inside of him and made it impossible to do anything. But he reminded himself that he was protected here. Still, he didn't answer. Hopefully, Eli would appear and help. He had to have known that this would happen to Tor.

Tor noticed someone walking along one of the paths that led to the ruins. "Tor?" the man called out. The man was dressed in a uniform of some sort. And he seemed averagely human.

As he stepped into the clearing, he saw Tor sitting on the ground. "Are you Tor?" he asked.

"Why?"

"I was sent by Timothy, the priest up at the abbey. He said you would be hungry and thirsty."

"Yes, thank you. You can set it there."

The man set the food down and handed Tor a canteen. "This is full of fresh water."

"Thank you." He opened it up and drank the cool liquid. Tor felt better.

"All right, I'll catch you around sometime." The guy said and headed toward the path he came from. He stopped and asked, "By the way, you wouldn't happen to know how to change a flat tire, do you? I need some help, and Timothy is busy at the abbey."

"How far are you?"

"Just right outside the forest. This path takes us right to the truck."

Tor felt the energy move through him. It acted like it was trying to communicate with him. "I'm not sure I know how."

"It's no problem if you can't. See you later."

This guy wasn't threatening at all, so why was Tor hesitating? "Wait up," he said. "I'll help."

He still couldn't push past some of the weakness, but he did sense he was stronger than when he first woke up to find Marcy there. Tor walked on the slight path just behind the uniformed man. "It's not too far from here. I'm really glad you can help. Delivery trucks are a pain when a tire goes flat."

The walk down the path took longer than Tor anticipated. He wished he could transport himself there, but he didn't have that ability anymore. Not yet, at any rate. As soon as the delivery driver exited the forest, Tor slowed down. He saw the truck. It was maybe

245

twenty feet from them. But he wondered if it was still on sacred land.

The man turned and gave Tor a questioning look. "It's just right here."

Tor glanced around. Nothing was out of the ordinary. He mentally shook himself and followed the delivery driver to the truck. When they reached it, Tor saw the flat tire. Good. At least the guy hadn't lied to him to lure him into a trap. They worked together to change the tire. Tor didn't necessarily have any experience, but having an extra pair of hands was all the guy needed. When they were finished, the man shook Tor's hand. "Thank you, man. God bless!" He slid into the truck's seat. "I would take you back, but this is too big of a truck."

"No problem. I can walk back." Tor watched the truck turn around and drive down the two-track road.

A chill shot up his spine, and he felt the all-too-familiar feeling of Drakkon. He had to be outside the boundaries. Moving as quickly as he could, he pushed himself to get to the forest.

But he didn't get very far. Drakkon stood in his way. "Hello, my son," he cooed. "Going somewhere?"

Tor froze, the fear immediately finding a place inside of him. But he wouldn't show it. "Drakkon. I wondered when you would finally find us."

"It was a bit more difficult than I had anticipated, especially since you haven't been reporting to me."

"How could I? I've been busy."

"You don't think I see what's happened to you?" Drakkon moved his wrist. Suddenly Tor's wrists and ankles were bound. "There, that's better."

Tor could feel hell's poisonous shackles eat at his skin. He gritted his teeth, refusing to show pain.

"You're weak," Drakkon said in disgust. "They made you weak. Is that what you *want*?" he bellowed, turning into the red dragon. He grabbed Tor in his mouth and flew out of the area.

The poison worked its way slowly through his veins. He only hoped that it would kill him before Drakkon could carry out whatever torturous plans he had devised.

When Drakkon landed, it was in the middle of a cemetery, still within the vicinity of the small town that housed the abbey. Tor tried to pay attention to direction, but the poison had him going in and out of consciousness.

Drakkon dropped Tor out of his mouth. Tor smacked his head against a gravestone, making him grimace in pain.

"Are they back?" Drakkon asked someone. Tor tried to get a good look, but he was still seeing stars.

"Not yet. I'm surprised to see you so soon."

"They stripped him of his powers." Drakkon turned to Tor. "There wasn't even a fight. Pathetic. But that's okay. He wasn't the one we wanted anyway."

"You think this could work?"

Tor saw the Shadow talking with Drakkon. Then he realized who it was.

Kraal.

"Don't ask stupid questions," Drakkon said to Kraal. He turned his attention to Tor and watched him. With absolute, unbridled hatred. "Look at you. All that work and you're stripped of everything. Those light-bearers think they're kind spirits. They don't take something unless it's asked of them. Is that what happened?" He took a step closer to Tor.

"I told him to kill me," Tor spat out, refusing to look away from Drakkon. "I asked him to end my miserable existence because I'd rather be dead than be a slave."

"A slave? I would have given you everything. Hadn't I promised you the throne?"

"Not like you to ever lie," Tor said sarcastically.

Drakkon paced back and forth. "They should be here by now."

"Want me to go check?"

"No. I want you to stay here and see what happens to those who double-cross me."

Kraal glanced from Drakkon to Tor then back to Drakkon. "I have never double-crossed you, sir. If it wasn't for me, you wouldn't have access to her unmatched power to begin with."

Drakkon wasn't listening. He still watched Tor. "I could have used both of you if you would have followed through." Drakkon stepped closer to Tor, closing the gap between them. Drakkon might have been standing, but Tor had no strength to stand. So,

Drakkon stooped down to get in Tor's face. "I asked you to break her. It was a simple request. Break her to enslave her. But no. What happened? Did the sway of her hips lure you in? Her feminine scent? Her flirty eyes?"

Death was imminent, but he refused to be intimidated anymore. "She wasn't like you."

Drakkon hit him with such force, that he heard the break of his nose before he felt the pain. But Drakkon wasn't done. He beat Tor, one blow after another. "You're worthless," he seethed, kicking him near the sword's scar. Tor couldn't keep it in, yelping in pain. "Yes, cry out, feed me with your agony."

The beating would have continued, but Kraal interrupted. "They're here."

Right before Tor lost all consciousness, he saw Marcy step out from a shadow.

29

Deborah

Marcy once again stood at the edge of the cliff. She took a deep breath and prepared herself for the fall.

"I don't think this is a good idea," Timothy said from behind her. "Michael already tried. You don't remember flying."

"I didn't have sufficient motivation," Marcy answered. "Besides, Michael isn't here to stop me. And I need to do something. I can't stand around and wait for the bad news."

"You don't know if it's bad news yet."

Marcy glanced down at the water. "Yes, Timothy, I do."

It took Marcy about sixty seconds after Michael and Eli left again to locate Tor that Marcy decided she needed to start remembering some things. Like flying. Even if Tor had left on his own—which she had a strong premonition wasn't the case—her duty involved protecting him. And she wasn't about to fail again.

The only reason she was listening at all to Michael and staying put was because in her current state she wouldn't be successful against the likes of Drakkon. She knew that. But it didn't make it easy. She needed to *remember*.

Before Michael left to pursue Tor, she promised him that it wouldn't be like last time. She wouldn't make any rash decisions without talking first to him. It was the least she could do after all of his sacrifice. But she didn't consider falling off a cliff a rash decision. More like a necessary one.

She outstretched her hands, closed her eyes, and started to fall. Fly, fly, fly.

"Marcy?" the voice called her name from far off.

She stopped and regained balance, turning quickly at the sound of the voice.

"Did you hear that?" she asked Timothy.

"Marcy?" the voice acted desperate. "Help me!"

"Mathilde?" Marcy stepped away from the cliff and scanned the landscape.

"Who's Mathilde?" Timothy asked.

Marcy started running in the direction of the voice. Timothy grabbed her arm. "No, Deborah, please. Whatever's happening might be a trick. Please don't leave."

"Marcy!" the girl cried. "He's going to kill us both!"

Movement caught Marcy's attention. Mathilde was shifting from shadow to shadow just outside the abbey. "She won't be able to enter," Marcy said, thinking to herself. To Timothy, she asked, "Those are still sacred grounds out there, right?"

"Yes, but…"

"How can she be on the sacred grounds, but not be able to pass through to the abbey?"

"Is she human?"

"Partly."

"That's why. That's why Tor was able to be on them. But the darkness in her does not allow her to enter through the holy place."

"But I could."

"After you shed the darkness. And even that, Michael took a risk."

"I need to go check on her." Timothy went to protest. Marcy added, "I will stay within the threshold."

Marcy ran across the open landscape of the abbey toward the outer gates where the Celtic crosses stood. "Mathilde!" she called out.

The young teen stopped moving. That was when Marcy saw the burn marks. And Mathilde's left arm had been completely singed off. Marcy slowed as she neared her friend, unable to hide the emotion. She covered her mouth as she walked the rest of the way to her. "Oh, Mathilde. What has he done to you?"

Mathilde might have only been a young teenager, but her face looked haggard. "I've been tortured as soon as Drakkon realized he had been tricked."

Marcy shook her head back and forth. "I'm so sorry," she whispered.

Now Mathilde's features twisted into a sneer. "Sorry? Really? You don't look sorry, Marcy. You look amazing. And that's nice. While you've been running around, I've been thrown in the cage over the inferno, and as soon as Rakye is done healing from his injuries, I'll be given over to him as a consolation prize. Thanks to you."

"You have to see I didn't want any of this to happen."

"What did you expect would happen, Marcy?" Mathilde yelled. "You left me there. To be tortured. To be burned. To be thrown into a cage."

"What do you need me to do? I can help you, Mathilde."

"He's going to kill me," she said. She took her one hand and rubbed her brow. "Tor's probably already dead. Drakkon was furious at him. But if I don't bring you back to see Drakkon, I will die after Rakye devours me."

"Tor?" Marcy said in a panic. "Drakkon's got Tor?" And there it was. Drakkon understood what truly motivated Marcy. *Love.* Drakkon would use it to his advantage. First with Mathilde and now with Tor. "Of course, I'll go see him." Marcy stepped across the threshold. She heard Timothy yelling in the distance, but she ignored him. Instead, she wrapped her arms around the girl who she abandoned.

Mathilde stiffened and stepped back. "It's too late for hugs, Marcy."

"I will do whatever I can to make this up to you."

The young teen's face became hard as she stepped into a shadow. "Follow me," she said with no emotion at all.

Marcy didn't think twice. She stepped into a shadow and followed her trainee.

The farther she traveled from the abbey, the more she felt the evil. It was tangible as if it traveled beside her. Marcy's gut told her that this wouldn't end well. But what choice did she have? She had sworn to protect Tor, and now he was in Drakkon's clutches. And she should have protected Mathilde. The failure nearly suffocated her. Could she do anything right?

The energy revolted inside her as she moved from shadow to shadow. Michael had been right; it was a dark practice. But she couldn't fly, and she didn't know how else to keep up with Mathilde.

"If only I could remember me as Deborah," she said out loud. From what everyone had told her, she had been a fierce warrior. Drakkon wouldn't stand a chance. But nope. She was clothed in Marcy's humanity. That meant defeating Drakkon would be next to impossible.

They were close. She sensed him. Her energy banged against the shell of her body warning her.

Then she saw Tor. Lying on the ground, so covered in blood that she wouldn't have recognized him if her heart hadn't told her it was him.

"Well, look who it is," Drakkon said with a wicked smile.

The energy roared in Marcy's ears almost to the point that she couldn't hear him. But she was too focused on Kraal, standing off to the side, to pay too much attention to Drakkon.

"Hello, Kraal," she said, her words like steel.

He looked away. Of course. Coward.

"She is a nice little pet, isn't she?"

Marcy turned her attention back to Drakkon and saw he had his hand around Mathilde's neck. "Let her go. She brought me here, didn't she?"

"Let her go? Never. I think I'm going to keep her as a pet. Put a collar around her neck. Feed her my scraps."

Mathilde whimpered.

"Stop!" Marcy yelled. The energy of the word roared through the cemetery. Drakkon dropped Mathilde, his eyes widened in surprise. "Tell me what it is you want, Drakkon. I have no time for your games."

"Incredible," Drakkon said, somewhat mystified. To Kraal, he said, "Imagine what we will be able to do with that power." He walked slowly over to Marcy. "Here's my proposition. Pledge your service to me. With your real blood, of course. This time you do it right."

"Why would I ever agree to do that?" The energy was so out-of-control inside Marcy, that she thought she might get sick.

"Because if you don't, I will kill Tor. Slowly, of course. And this little Shadow girl? I will throw her into the inferno as was promised many days ago."

"Marcy…don't listen to him," words escaped Tor's mouth.

"Wait, my deal gets better," Drakkon said. "I'll even let you and Tor be together for eternity. Yes, that's right. No interference from me. Your real boyfriend won't mind, will he?"

Marcy saw Tor shake his head. She looked over at Mathilde who still whimpered.

"Oh, and don't try anything," Drakkon said. "This cemetery contains some of the fiercest demons in hell. Upon my command, I will unleash them. I might not be able to kill you, but this entire mortal community will be destroyed in seconds."

She couldn't see any way around it. An eternity of servitude to the master of darkness. Marcy wondered what Michael would do when he found out. For a brief moment, her heart panged at the thought of hurting him. His kindness and protection had been a welcomed relief. She longed to get to know him all over again, to remember their closeness. But right now, Tor and Mathilde needed her.

"Release them," she said.

"Excuse me?"

"If you want me to sign, you will free them of service to you. And they will not be touched at all by hell. Ever again." Marcy stared at Drakkon with such intensity that even he looked away.

"Fine. Done. I never wanted Tor anyway. Kraal promised that if I kept the human boy under my wing that it would bring victory, especially when I saw hell's secret weapon in action."

Marcy glared at Kraal. "Yes, Kraal is very good at manipulating and lying. You should feel proud."

"I did what I had to do, Marcy," he said in desperation. "We need to win this war. I don't want to be enslaved forever."

"Winning the war isn't going to free you, Kraal. Drakkon is the one who is enslaving you. That's not going to change."

"All right, let's get on with it." A large book materialized and hovered in front of Marcy. She pressed against her stomach. The energy would not be quieted. Drakkon began, "I swear to the heavens that Tor and Mathilde will be free from hell, and they will never be touched by it again…"

"And Kraal…"

Drakkon stopped. Kraal watched Marcy in shock.

"If I'm doing this, you don't need Kraal anymore, right? So free him, too. Tor, Mathilde, and Kraal."

"No," Tor said from the ground. "Marcy, don't do this."

"Fine. All three of them are freed from hell in exchange for your eternal service."

"Agreed," Marcy whispered, swallowing back bile.

Drakkon yanked her arm and cut her palm with his nail. "Now sign," he hissed.

Marcy's hand trembled. The earth began to tremble. Thunder tore across the sky. Marcy knew that Michael had found out and was on his way.

"Hurry!" Drakkon shouted. "Or I kill them now!"

Marcy pressed her eyes together, bringing her hand down to the book. Suddenly, there was an explosion in her ears. It threw her across the cemetery. Images began to flood through her mind. Images of golden streets, perfect gardens, endless power, and love. Her heart soared with love. The kiss of an archangel. The promise of forever.

She heard screaming, but it seemed so far away. When Marcy opened her eyes, she drew in a surprised breath. She was in the air, far above the clouds. She glanced down and saw tiny specks. And she laughed.

Suddenly, Drakkon appeared beside her. "You're not the only one who can fly, Marcy," he said and grabbed her arm. "Now sign before it's too late!"

Marcy saw that her hand had already healed. She held it up for Drakkon to see. "Looks like I'll be unable to. And for the record, my name's not Marcy. It's Deborah." And she did what she had wanted to do for months. She punched Drakkon with every ounce of her angelic strength and sent him spiraling through the air.

Using those few moments, she flew back to the ground. It came easily to her, and she understood now that the energy inside of her had been pushing for its release. Now she felt the power of heaven at her fingertips.

She landed on the ground, shaking the earth from the impact. Drakkon had already released the demons. Many trembled when they saw her.

But Michael had arrived, already winning the fight. Deborah shot out energy, turning wild demons and imps to ash. Michael made eye contact with her and grinned. They fought together, as the demon onslaught continued.

"Where's Tor?" she asked Michael. He pointed to the other side of the cemetery.

"Go check on him. I've got this." He head-butted a demon, crippling it.

She flew above the cemetery, but she couldn't find him. "Tor?"

she called out, just hovering over the ground. "Tor?"

"Behind you!" Michael yelled.

Deborah spun around and used the energy to disintegrate an enormous demon she had never encountered before jumping up to grab her. Another dozen or two swarmed her, piling on top of each other to reach her. "I need a weapon!" she yelled. Sighing, she held out her hand and summoned a large stick. Any stick would do. It was in her hands in seconds.

One of the demons lunged at her; its mouth open, showing its hideous fangs. It snapped its jaws trying to bite her. She maneuvered the stick, sending with every hit the powerful energy inside of her. The monstrous demons didn't stand a chance.

"Got your weapon?" Michael asked.

"Yes." Deborah started smacking miniature imps with it, slicing through them. "But I need to get out of here. I can't find Tor."

A scream shook the air, as Michael and Deborah faced the red dragon.

"You want to fight me again?" Michael roared at Drakkon. "It didn't work out too well for you last time, but I have no problem taking up where we left off!"

"That's all right, I have a human to kill. I will kill them. All!" He disappeared through a blue mist.

"No!" Deborah wailed, flying toward the blue mist.

Michael grabbed her. "Don't do this again, Deborah. We will save him. I promise. But we do it together. We are unbeatable if we do not separate again."

She stopped struggling as the sobs took over. She might have remembered who she was, but once again, Deborah was at square one.

And Tor was in hell.

29

Departure

He saw the energy shoot out from Marcy and send her soaring into the air. And he smiled. Or at least he tried to.

That's when the chaos began, and, well, all hell broke loose.

Tor needed to get away before the onslaught of demons killed him, or worse, took him back to the one place he never wanted to see again. But he couldn't move. Not because his legs were injured, but the burning energy from the sword's wound had now traveled through his whole body, making him convulse. At the moment, that Eli guy was not on his favorites list. Not that he ever had one. He really could have used his powers to help Marcy and Lynde, or Deborah and Michael, whatever the heck their names were.

Two things he knew for certain, especially after watching her nearly sign her eternity away to Drakkon. He loved Marcy, loved her something fierce. But he also knew for certain that they would never be together. Simply being, that he could never be good enough for her. But he would have to deal with those feelings at a later time.

Suddenly, someone grabbed him from behind and placing their arms under his armpits, pulled him up. "Come on. We have to get out of here."

Kraal?

"No." Tor tried to fight, but he was completely without strength. "I can't go back there."

He hated the thought of begging, but images of torture flashed through his mind, and he didn't relish reliving any of that.

Kraal didn't listen and stepped into a shadow. He traveled fast, even with Tor leaning against him. Tor knew that once Shadows joined the ranks their skills developed quickly, and Kraal was no exception.

Suddenly he stepped out of the shadow. Tor felt a little woozy, but it could have been from a multitude of factors.

"Did you get anyone's attention?" Kraal asked.

"Huh?"

Tor then saw Mathilde standing along the edge of the forest. The same forest he had left when helping that guy change his tire. "What's going on?"

Mathilde ignored him. "I've been calling out, but I don't want to bring more attention to myself. We're already in so much trouble."

"We're not in trouble," Kraal clarified. "If we get captured, we're *dead*."

Eli appeared just inside the trees. "I'm here," he said to Mathilde and Kraal. "I cannot step out of this sanctuary. Darkness and light cannot mix."

"You need to hurry," Mathilde said to Kraal.

Kraal glanced at Tor and whispered, "Tell her to come back and save us." Then he took Tor and shoved him into the forest.

Eli caught Tor right when they heard a wretched scream fill the air.

"Come on," Kraal told Mathilde. "We need to hide."

"I can offer you sanctuary within these woods, but I will have to kill the demon within you," Eli said to them. "It will hurt…and I can't guarantee that you'll survive."

"I can't leave the other Shadows," Kraal said, the emotion showing on his face. "But we need help. Please. Tell the Nameless One that we will do whatever it takes. We're not entirely demon."

"I know." Eli had sadness in his voice.

"We're human, too. Please, just tell Marcy not to forget us. And tell her…" Kraal swallowed as if the words hurt him. "Tell her I only wanted to be free."

Tor looked at Kraal. "Thank you," he said. "When I gain strength, I will join her and free you all."

"Don't make a promise you cannot keep," Eli whispered to Tor.

"It's a promise I *intend* to keep. No one should be a slave. No one."

Kraal nodded, grabbed Mathilde's one good hand, and then they stepped into a shadow.

"When he finds them, he's going to kill them," Tor said.

Eli wrapped Tor's arm around his shoulders. "Hold on," he said, then moved them from the edge of the forest to the inside of his cave in under a second.

"I used to be able to do that," Tor muttered, as Eli set him on the same stone slab Tor had laid on before.

"You'll be able to do far more than that, but right now, you need to rest." Eli poured hot water from a kettle over the fire. "I have some herbal paste that'll help with your injuries."

"Do you have anything for the burning sensation that's happening inside of me?"

"No. But it's good that you're feeling it. It means it's accepted your body as its temple. I was worried that it wouldn't." He walked over and dipped a cloth into the hot water. "I've got to clean up the mess he made of your face. I could knock you out again. It'll probably be painful if you're conscious of it."

"I'll be fine." Tor gritted his teeth, as Eli got to work. As time passed, the only thing that kept Tor conscious was thoughts of her. "You should have seen it," he mumbled, almost deliriously. "She exploded. Sent him reeling. Bolts of light like lightning shot through her and pushed her up into the sky. I've never seen anything like it."

Eli stayed quiet and kept applying the herbal past to Tor's wounds.

"When he cut her palm, everything in me screamed against it. But I was useless to help. I don't know what I would have done if she had signed the book."

"Don't be too hard on yourself. It can't happen. Drakkon knows this. He probably assumed because the light-bearer was contained in a human shell that Deborah would be trapped within that body. But a light-bearer can never serve him. In an ironic turn of events what he meant to subject her to him, actually freed the light-bearer within her."

"So, she is a full-fledged angel?"

"Yes."

"No longer Marcy."

"No. The supernatural power destroyed the human shell. I believe she is a full angel now." Eli pushed himself back and looked at Tor. "Give it time and the wound will heal."

"Which wound?"

"All of them. Both external and internal."

"What if I proved myself to her? I've got this energy inside of me now. It feels powerful. I think I could…if I tried."

"You are not a light-bearer, Tor. You are a human. A human with amazing gifts, one who has been chosen to lead mankind against the torrent of hell that's coming. But Deborah and Michael are archangels."

"Does she remember now? Remember her feelings for Michael?"

"Probably. That doesn't mean she has forgotten you, but love feels different depending on the relationship."

"She said she loves me but not in the way I'd want."

"Considering how in love she was with Michael, I'm not surprised. I'm not sure how any of it is going to play out if there is some sort of love triangle."

"There's not going to be any triangle," Tor said, hiding the emotion he felt. He knew what he had to do. He had to step away from the equation. He knew it, but his heart panged at the thought of never having her in his arms. But as much as his need and desire for Marcy—or Deborah now—his brain also knew that he wasn't the best match for her. And the plain and simple truth remained that she and Michael were an item long before he entered the picture. A part of him simply didn't care about any of that. Michael and Deborah's past relationship was just that—it was in the past. But he refused to be the third wheel.

"Don't do that," Eli said, handing him a container of water. "Don't think about anything other than getting rest. You were seriously knocking on death's door and are only about a step or two further away from it now."

Tor drank the water and laid back down. A shadow covered the sun from the cave's opening. He turned and could make out Marcy standing there, watching him with concern but also complete relief on her face.

"You're here." She rushed over to him. "I was going to the abbey, but I wanted to stop here to double-check. I was already grieving that you were back in hell."

"Well, I'm here. No need to grieve."

"Look at you," she whispered, touching his hair.

Her touch sent a torch through his body. Why did it have to be this way? "That bad, huh?" he croaked out.

She smiled sadly. "Once again, I nearly lost you," she said, unable to hide what was troubling her. "What would I have done?"

"You didn't lose me. I'm here. Eli's helping me. You should get back to Michael."

"Trust me, Mike's fine. He's finishing up the last of the demons and told me to go on ahead of him."

"Mike?"

"Yeah," she said, her grin widening. "Turns out, that's what I call him."

The ground beneath them shook, and then Michael entered the cave.

"Show off," Marcy teased him.

Michael smiled at her before taking a look at Tor. It was the first time Tor had seen him as a light-bearer. Tor had never—ever—felt intimidated. Well, not since the torture sessions of his youth. Until this moment. Michael was hands-down the fiercest warrior Tor had ever seen. Had he tried to fight him? It was clear that Michael must have let Tor beat up on him because Tor had heard the legends of the angel warrior who battled Drakkon in hell…and won. "How are you doing?" Michael asked him.

Embarrassment heated his face. Only human. He clenched his fists at the thought. "Don't look at me with concern," Tor said, turning his face to the cave's wall. He couldn't take it. He couldn't take the look of sympathy on that light-bearer's face. And did he have to look perfect? At least before, Lynde had been gruesome and flat-out ugly. Tor felt human. Pathetically human. He felt a twinge of anger at Eli. At least before, he had his powers. He might have been stupid, even then, for thinking he could stand a chance, but he would take that cockiness now over this limp, nearly dead, human body.

"Broken ribs, broken nose, broken heart," Eli said to Michael.

"If you guys don't shut it," Tor said, but he didn't know how to finish it. It wasn't like he was any threat. "The minute I can, I'm out of here," he promised himself.

"Tor, please don't turn away," Marcy whispered. "You're important to us."

Us? Great.

"Could you give me a minute with him?" Michael asked.

Tor grunted. Great. That's exactly what he needed. Alone time with the big guy.

He still faced the wall, but he could feel Michael step closer and stand over him. Whatever burning energy was happening inside of him started trembling as the archangel came closer.

"Tor," Michael said quietly. When Tor didn't respond, he continued, "I don't want to fight you."

That statement made Tor want to explode. Mostly because Tor wanted nothing more than to fight, but he couldn't. He wanted to fight for the woman he loved. He wanted to prove that he could be good enough for her. It might be futile, but he desired nothing more than to fight, even if the fight would most definitely result in him losing. If that wasn't bad enough, he already owed Michael a debt he could never pay. If it wasn't for him disguising himself, Marcy would have been stuck in hell with Tor, a vengeful, angry monster who had no problem following evil orders that included killing her and even manipulating her. And yet, Michael rescued them both.

Maybe Tor should have said thank you, but he didn't feel like it. It's not like he was a perfect angel or anything.

"I'm glad you weren't taken back there. To that horrible place."

"Me too," Tor admitted. "Kraal and Mathilde brought me here while the fight was happening."

"That was kind of them."

"They long to be free." Tor finally looked at Michael. "I'm glad she found out who she really is."

"Me too."

"It doesn't make it easier, but it's what needed to happen."

"There's one more thing you should know," Michael said. "It's about your father."

Tor turned to lay flat and winced at the pain. "What about him?"

"He'd like to see you."

Tor's heart quickened. "My father? He's here?"

"He's close. I didn't want to say anything earlier because I didn't think you were ready for everything to be thrown at you."

"I want to see him. And my mother?"

Michael looked away. "From what I heard, the grief killed her."

Tor pressed his lips together, letting his own grief consume him. "I sometimes hear her sing."

"She was a gifted human and a heart for goodness. She's one of us now. That's why your father stays at the abbey. He devoted his life to service of the Most High so that he can be reunited with her when the time comes."

Tor had so much to process. "I need to be left alone, please."

Michael nodded, and he turned to leave.

"So, were you faking it?"

Michael looked back at Tor. "Faking what?"

"When we fought…were you faking weakness?"

Michael didn't respond.

"So, you could have annihilated me? You know, you're really killing my ego."

"Good. Egos are dangerous."

"Whatever. You can leave now."

Michael watched him for a moment longer before stepping out of the cave.

Tor stared up at the cave's ceiling and took in deep breaths. Too much. How was he supposed to handle all of this? His father was around, but his mother was dead. Marcy was now some fierce archangel, and Michael had somehow managed to save his life, get him to safety, and steal the girl. How could appreciation and annoyance be brewing in the same pot? "Eli?" he called out. "Are you around?"

Eli appeared on the other side of the fire. "When you're in this forest, I'm always around. I thought you wanted to be alone?"

"I needed him to leave."

"It's funny, isn't it? That the big tough guy standing outside of this cave can have no guile in him. That the only thing he hates is evil. And that he will do whatever it takes to bring you and the one he loves to safety, even if it means enduring the place he reviles the most, pretending to blend in a world that is the exact counter to who he is."

"He went there for her. I'm the door prize."

"He went there for both of you. If Deborah had waited before impulsively striking a deal with Kraal, the both of them could have come up with a plan to bring you back. But you were always the objective. Always. He would not have left without you. Who do you think put the idea in Drakkon's mind for you to watch Marcy as her Guardian? Who do you think put the idea in his head for you to travel with them to train?"

"Okay, I get it. You're in the 'Michael' fan club. Never mind." Tor thought for a moment, then added, "Why didn't he just storm in there and rip us both out? He could take on the entire legions of hell."

"You know why. Light-bearers would easily be seen. And even though he is invincible, he did not know if Marcy was. Camouflaging herself as a human could have made her fragile. And he already knew that you were human and not invincible. If he showed himself, Drakkon could have easily killed you both. Michael couldn't take that chance."

Tor finally said the words that had been replaying over and over in his head since he was first dropped off. "I need to leave."

"That's not possible."

"Eli, please." Tor pushed himself up, grimacing from shooting pains that reminded him of his humanity. Still, he sat up and stared at Eli with the one eye that had not swollen shut. "You know that I cannot have her. And even though I…*appreciate*…what Michael has done, I will constantly feel as if I am in his shadow. From the sound of it, I have some capabilities that I need to practice and develop. If I can get away and do that, then maybe she will fade in my heart, or at the very least I can work through the emotions of having to let her go."

Eli studied Tor for several minutes. "There is a place. But you'd have to get permission."

"From who?"

Eli cocked his head to the side and stared at Tor with raised eyebrows. Tor sighed.

"All right, send him back in."

A moment later, Michael entered without Eli moving, which meant he was listening. Tor pushed down the annoyance. "Glad to see you giving me privacy."

"I did. Eli told me to come back in."

Tor looked at both of them. "Fine. I don't care. I just need to know if I can go to someplace…away from here…away from her…and develop whatever gifts I've got going on."

"Will you tell her?"

"No, and you can't tell her where I'm at either. It's better this way. I need to focus…" *and stop thinking about her,* but Tor didn't say the last part.

"You'll need someone to go with you," Michael said. "And I know just the person who will want the job."

Tor nodded, knowing exactly who Michael was referring to. "It's about time I meet my father anyway. When do I leave?"

30

Beginning Again

She stood at the edge of the waterfall, staring out at the horizon, trying to compartmentalize all of the memories that had come flooding back. She knew who she was. No longer Marcy. No longer a scared young woman, no longer a confused and angry Shadow trainee, no longer a highly volatile human. She was Deborah, the archangel sworn to protect the child who would grow up to help mankind survive the soon-to-be Armageddon.

And yet…

She turned and looked back at the cave. She remembered now the intense love she had for Michael. But Tor complicated things. How could she love a human and an archangel? With Tor out of hell, he would need to be a priority. Where did that leave her relationship with Michael? They had over twenty mortal years to catch up on.

Just then, Michael stepped out of the cave. He looked at her and smiled. She smiled before turning to look again at the horizon.

"He's still angry with me," Michael said as he came up beside her.

"He's had a lot thrown at him," she said. "Then on top of all that, Drakkon beat him within an inch of his life."

"That's not why he's angry with me," Michael said quietly.

Deborah felt the pang in her heart. "I know. I do love him."

"I know," Michael said quietly. "I will not interfere if that is what you'd like."

"What I'd like? I'd like our twenty years back, but they're gone. All this time I never truly saw what was in front of my eyes. I never saw you, but now that my eyes have been opened, I never want to look away again. What I'd like is *you*."

Michael breathed a sigh of relief, nodding slowly. "How much do you remember?"

"All of it. But it's weird. I have all of Deborah's experiences and all of Marcy's."

"Do you remember us?" She felt his hand in hers. Deborah glanced down at their intertwined fingers, then glanced up at Michael.

"I do." She reached up and touched his face, caressing it. He closed his eyes and kissed her palm. Butterflies released again inside of her. "This feeling, this love, is so powerful. Is this what you felt for twenty years without being able to express it?"

"Our love kept me going," he said, leaning his forehead onto hers. "It gave me hope."

"Thank you for not giving up on me."

"Never."

"Michael?"

"Hmm?"

"You said you wouldn't kiss me until I asked."

Our gaze met, and in that moment, he took my breath away. "Are you asking?"

Marcy nodded, unable to find words. Michael brought his lips to hers, and warmth flooded through her entire body like warm honey to weary bones. And in this moment, she finally felt home.

Michael and Deborah stayed that way for some time, delighting in their renewed love until Michael looked back at the cave. "Tor wants to see me." He dropped Deborah's hand. "I'll be right back."

Deborah waited until he was in the cave, then she closed her eyes and smiled. Tor was safe, and all of her memories had returned. It had always been Michael, but for twenty years, she was oblivious. Taking a deep breath, she flew straight up, letting the chilly air embrace her. "Thank you," she said to the sky, knowing He heard.

When Deborah stepped foot back on the ground, the sun had already set, and the moon and stars had taken their place in the sky.

She decided to go check on Tor before heading back to the abbey. She reasoned that it was only showing concern, nothing more.

Eli stepped out of the cave. "He's not here," he said.

"Michael or Tor?"

"Tor."

"Tor's not here? Where is he?"

"With Michael."

"Oh, are they at the abbey?"

"No."

Deborah paused. "Okay, then where are they?"

"I don't know. It's a secret location where Tor can heal and then train properly. No one is supposed to know. Only Michael knows, and he's taking him there." Eli shrugged.

Secret location? Deborah tried to think of the secret locations she knew of. Only a few came to mind. She remembered there being many more that Michael was responsible for. Since her job had been to oversee these sacred grounds, she hadn't needed to know about others. "Well, that's good, right?"

"I think so, yes. He appears to be in a hurry to get his powers back."

Deborah understood that Tor had purposefully left without saying goodbye. It was easier this way. This was his way of putting distance between them.

"He made me promise to tell you about Kraal and Mathilde."

Deborah's breath caught. "What about them?" She had wondered since the battle where they had gone, or if they had been killed. She didn't want her brain to go there, so she instead focused on Tor's broken condition.

"They brought Tor back here."

"They did?"

"Yes, and Kraal asked Tor to tell you not to forget about them. I offered for them to come in here, but they did not want to forsake the other Shadows and trainees."

Deborah brought a hand to her heart. "They feel I've forsaken them."

"I don't think so. I only think that they don't want you to forget. They need your help, or they will all die."

Mathilde's words and anger came flooding back. "Drakkon will kill them."

"Don't get any ideas. Wait for Michael. Saving an entire species from hell, many of which probably do not desire to be saved, is going to be a difficult feat."

Deborah nodded and waved goodbye at Eli. She flew up and over the trees and headed toward the abbey. She loved flying. Forget shadow jumping. But that thought brought her to Mathilde and Kraal. If they brought Tor back, then they were probably on the run, hiding somewhere here on earth. It would only be a matter of time before they're found.

Deborah touched the ground and walked into the abbey. "Timothy?" she called out. The abbey was quiet. That only made the itch to do something that much more powerful.

Not even an hour passed before Deborah thought she'd lose her mind from the quiet. She decided that she would case out the area, only to see if there might be any clues to where Kraal and Mathilde went. Up in the air, she would be undetected. And she doubted Drakkon would come close right now. She walked outside and right into Michael.

"Hey, where are you off to?"

"Michael," she breathed his name, unable to contain her joy at seeing him again. She stood on her tiptoes and kissed him. "I missed you. I was getting ready to check the area."

"And I missed you. And this." He kissed her again.

"Where is Timothy?" she asked, enjoying the sensation of being in Michael's arms.

"Timothy's with Tor. He'll be good for him."

"You can't tell me, can you? Where they went?"

"Tor asked me not to or else I would."

"It's probably for the best." She said the words, but she didn't know if she entirely meant them.

Michael studied her silently.

"What?"

He shook his head. "I just can't believe that you are finally here. In my arms. The real you."

Her worry over Tor paused at Michael's sincere words. She leaned into him, closing her eyes for a moment. "Why do I feel I'm not entirely complete?"

"You will be, but you are concerned for others. We have loose ends to figure out and fix."

"I need to make sure that Kraal and Mathilde are safe."

"Don't forget they're still agents of hell."

"Not by their own volition. They saved Tor. What agent in hell would do that?"

"Maybe agents with an agenda."

"I don't see it that way."

"I know you don't." He kissed her gently on the lips. "And I love you for it."

Deborah sighed, "They are slaves, Mike. Plus, they're my friends, or at the very least, they were the two I was closest with when I was in hell. I can't abandon them. I don't think He would want me to, at least that's what I sense."

Michael looked up at the sky, then back at Deborah. "So, what's your plan?"

That surprised her. Deborah fumbled a response, "Um, I hadn't got that far yet."

"You said something about checking out the area?"

"Yes, to see if there are any clues."

"Sounds like a good place to start." He extended his hand.

"You'll go with me?"

Michael smiled gently at her. "We're a team. I'm with you every step of the way. Even if it means another trip to hell."

Gratitude poured over Deborah like a warm rain. Of course, he'd be with her. Constant, faithful Michael. She hadn't realized how little she desired to be alone. Sure, she might be the fierce Deborah, but she hadn't relished the idea of fighting Drakkon without help. "Thank you." Taking Michael's hand, they flew into the night sky.

The End of Book I

Find out what happens to Tor and the others in Book II:

Guardians of the Mortal Realm

Acknowledgments

Thank you, first and foremost, to the Creator of all life and all good things. Every blessing I have comes from God, and I'm forever grateful.

Thank you to my family for their encouragement during the years it took to right this book (and all the others I wrote). I appreciate your patience with me when I ask for just five more minutes.

Everyone needs a friend like Rachel Anderson. She is my kindred spirit, editor, and prayer partner. She has read multiple versions of this book (and all my other books too). Thank you, my friend.

To everyone else who has been a supporter of my writing endeavors: thank you. I'm glad my book made it into your hands.

Blessings,

Shay Lee

Thank you for reading

Shadows of the Mortal Realm

Be looking for the next two books in the

***Mortal Realm* series:**

Guardians of the Mortal Realm

Warriors of the Mortal Realm

Other highly-acclaimed novels by

Shay Lee Giertz:

Falling Too Deep

Lake of Secrets